A SEASON AT BRIGHTON

The Eversley Saga Book Three

Alice Chetwynd Ley

SAPERE BOOKS

Also in The Eversley Saga
The Clandestine Betrothal
The Toast of the Town
An Eligible Gentleman

A SEASON AT BRIGHTON

Published by Sapere Books.

20 Windermere Drive, Leeds, England, LS17 7UZ,
United Kingdom

saperebooks.com

Copyright © The Estate of Alice Chetwynd Ley, 1971.

The Estate of Alice Chetwynd Ley has asserted their right to be identified as the author of this work.

All rights reserved.

No part of this publication may be reproduced, stored in any retrieval system, or transmitted, in any form, or by any means, electronic, mechanical, photocopying, recording, or otherwise, without the prior written permission of the publishers.
This book is a work of fiction. Names, characters, businesses, organisations, places and events, other than those clearly in the public domain, are either the product of the author's imagination, or are used fictitiously.
Any resemblances to actual persons, living or dead, events or locales are purely coincidental.

ISBN: 978-1-912546-63-3

*To Katie,
the delightful daughter I gained*

Chapter I: Lady in Distress

The brightness of a summer sunset filled the sky as a smart yellow curricle drawn by two fine bay horses drew up before an inn on the road to Cuckfield. The driver, a slim, elegant man in his late twenties, jumped down, closely followed by the boy who sat perched up behind him. An ostler, carelessly lounging against the stable door, threw away the straw he had been chewing, and hurried forward.

"A tankard of ale I must have, Jack, before we cover another mile," declared the gentleman to the boy, in a pleasant, quiet drawl. "You'll want one yourself — be back in fifteen minutes."

He tossed a coin, which the boy caught neatly.

"Thank ye, m'Lud. But ye knows very well that I never touches spirituous liquors."

The gentleman raised a quizzical eyebrow, and the ostler, who was holding the horses' heads, gaped at the lad in astonishment.

"I was forgetting your convictions for the moment. Perhaps they'll give you some tea or coffee in the kitchen instead."

He swung into the inn with a graceful, long-legged stride. It was a low-ceilinged building of Tudor times, and the traveller had to duck his head as he passed into the coffee room, which was empty at present. He was soon joined by the landlord, who took the modest order and went away to fetch it, leaving the guest to stare from the window at the beauty of the evening sky, with its massed clouds of rose and gold.

At such moments, in contemplation of Nature's daily yet ever-changing spectacle, a man feels at peace. The road had been hot and dusty; the first deep draught at the tankard eased his parched throat and contributed to his sense of well-being. It was almost with a feeling of outrage, therefore, that he gradually became conscious of a disturbance going on outside the door of the coffee room.

He tried to ignore it at first, reluctant to have his peace shattered; but soon the raised voices became so penetrating that he could not possibly avoid overhearing.

"No, I won't — I won't!" It was a young girl's voice, raised in a half-demented shriek. "It's all lies he's telling you, landlord — I swear I never saw him before in all my life until half an hour ago, when he gave me a lift on the road!"

"Take no notice." A rich, plummy, assured voice came next to the solitary traveller's ears. "I tell you, she's often like this, poor soul — too much inbreeding in the family, I dare say."

"You know nothing of my family!" screamed the girl. "Don't listen to him, landlord! My father's Sir George Denham, and he'll pay you well if you save me from this — this monster! He's not my husband — he's *not*, he's *not* — I swear it! Look — see — there's no ring on my finger! See for yourself!"

The plummy voice gave a rumbling laugh. "She's always throwing off her wedding ring — costs me a fortune keeping her supplied with 'em. Now, my pretty ladybird, come along upstairs —"

There were sounds of a brief struggle punctuated by shrieks. Above this, the landlord's troubled tones sounded: "Well, y'r honour, I don't rightly know — I don't want any disturbance in my house. Maybe I'd better ask y'r honour to find accommodation elsewhere, seeing as y'r good lady's so noisy — there, now! The poor dear's fainted."

There was silence for a moment, then the plummy voice said: "Damnation! Where's the nearest doctor?"

8

"Not till Cuckfield," replied the landlord. "But there's no need of a doctor, y'r honour — I'll fetch my missus, she'll soon bring her to. Nothing like a woman to deal with these little female ailments."

"Well, do what you can, but I'll fetch a doctor just the same."

The traveller in the coffee room heard the slam of the inn door as someone went out. A moment later, the door of his retreat was pushed open and the landlord entered, carrying in his arms an unconscious young woman whom he carefully deposited on an oak settle which flanked the large open fireplace.

The traveller pushed away his tankard, flung down a coin, and jumped to his feet. Now that his moment of contemplation had been disturbed, there was no point in staying. He glanced briefly at the girl lying on the settle, her warm brown hair flowing about her. He frowned. It was some years since he had seen any of Sir George Denham's young ladies, but this one certainly had the family features. There had been six girls, he remembered, but no heir. He had certainly never heard of there being any insanity in the family — that was ridiculous.

"Sad — sad," muttered the landlord, moving towards the door. "I'll just fetch my missus, y'r honour, an' then I'll be back in a jiffy if there's anything more ye're wantin'."

"No, thanks, I'm off," replied the traveller, but his words were cut short by the door closing.

Before he turned to follow the landlord, he gave one more look at the girl. Yes, she had the Denham nose, right enough; she was not precisely a beauty, but decidedly attractive, her face soft and demure in repose, as now. Was it fancy, or had he seen one eye open quickly, then shut again? He lingered, staring down at her.

Suddenly she opened both eyes very wide, leapt up from the settle, looked distractedly round the room and exclaimed: "Help me to hide!"

He shook his head, turning towards the door. "I fear I cannot intrude myself on your affairs, madam."

"Oh, but you must!" She flung herself upon him, dragging at the sleeve of his coat. "You have the look of a gentleman — you'll not let that horrible creature get hold of me again —"

"You refer to your husband?"

"Husband!" She spat out the word. "He's no more my husband than — than you are! He's just someone who offered to give me a lift to my home, when — when I was stranded, without money! And like a fool, I trusted him, never thinking he would try to — try —" Her voice tailed off for a moment, then came back more strongly as she exclaimed, vehemently: "Oh, how I *hate* Viscount Pamyngton! All this is his fault, really!"

The gentleman had begun to disentangle himself gently but firmly from her grasp, but at this he paused.

"Pamyngton?" he queried. "What has he to do with your concerns, ma'am?"

"Oh, no matter — forget I spoke his name — I am so distracted, I don't know what I'm saying! Only I am *not* mad, as that dreadful creature pretends I am! Please, please, help me to hide somewhere so that he can't find me when he returns! I am quite unprotected — and I forgot to bring any money — but my father is Sir George Denham, of Eastridge House — if only you will help me to hide until that man goes away for good, perhaps I'll be able to persuade the innkeeper to send me home in one of his chaises. Please, please help me!"

At this moment, the innkeeper and his wife came into the room.

"So the lady's better, is she?" asked the landlady, a trace of acidity in her tone. "Well, ma'am, a fine to-do there's been on your account, an' no mistake! But I'm thinkin', ma'am, as we'll need to ask ye both to find some other shelter for the night. This has always been a quiet, respectable house — and we'd like to keep it so."

"But I tell you that man is not my husband —"

The landlady drew herself up. "All the worse for both of ye," she said, forthrightly. "And that makes matters simpler. Out ye go, the moment he gets back."

"But I don't want to be here when he comes back," said the girl, with a helpless gesture of her shapely white hands. "You don't understand. I don't know him at all — he picked me up on the road a few miles back —"

"Indeed!" snorted the landlady, arms akimbo. "And to look at ye, I'd think ye were the Quality! Well, no tellin' how they'll behave, I suppose, any more than other folk."

"Please believe me," pleaded the girl, tossing her thick brown hair from her face. "If you'll let me have a carriage to take me home, my father will pay the charges at the other end."

The woman shook her head. "If ye'll tell one story, ye'll tell another. Anyways, we can't, because all our carriages is out on hire already. No, the most I can do is to let ye wait here until your — well, whatever he is," she finished, scathingly, "comes back for ye. I'm sorry, but there it is."

She elevated her nose, and pushed her husband out of the room.

"I never heard anything less like remorse," said the gentleman, quietly, when the door had closed upon the pair.

The girl did not answer, but flung herself on the settle and buried her face in her hands. He saw that her shoulders were shaking.

He sighed. He never seemed able to avoid involving himself in other people's troubles for long.

"Don't distress yourself, madam," he said, gently. "I rather fancy your cavalier of the road won't return at all."

She raised her head and a gleam of hope shone in the tear-misted eyes. "Oh, do you really think so? He said he was going to fetch a doctor."

A look of amusement crossed his face. "Then you heard what was said? You weren't unconscious?"

"Of course not! But it was all I could think of to do."

She sniffed delicately, and hunted about her for a handkerchief. He drew one from his pocket, and handed it to her silently.

"Thank you." She mopped at her eyes for a few moments, then absent-mindedly stuffed the handkerchief into a reticule which swung from her wrist.

"But what shall I do now?" she asked, helplessly. "I am miles from home — too far to walk — and I have no money, even supposing I could find somewhere to hire a carriage."

"I think," he said, looking at her gravely, "you must allow me to escort you home."

She started up, full of eagerness. "Oh, would you?" Then her face fell. "But no, that's what happened before. I thought *he* was a gentleman, too. It never crossed my mind that he would — would try to play me such a trick, or nothing would have induced me to step up into his carriage. No, it will not do, sir. Perhaps I am doing you an injustice, but you must see that I cannot risk such a thing happening again."

"Perhaps I should tell you," he said, with a smile, "that I am closely related to the Bishop of Standean, a circumstance that has always exercised, alas, a most beneficial effect on my conduct. Furthermore, we shall be chaperoned on our journey to your home by my tiger, Jack, a prodigiously strait-laced lad. I think he's of the Methodist persuasion, so you will have the protection of both the Established and the Nonconformist churches, so to speak."

She looked at him steadily, trying to assess him. It was almost a handsome face, with good features and dark blue eyes that could, she was certain, be very expressive. At present, they only showed amusement; but there was a gentleness about the mouth that reassured her. He stood patiently still under her scrutiny.

"Well, have you decided to trust me?" he asked. "By the way, perhaps I should also mention that I am acquainted with your family."

"Are you indeed?" She jumped up quickly. "Oh, well, that makes it all right, of course! Thank goodness, for I was almost at my wits' end, I can tell you! Pray, what is your name, sir?"

"It is Gerard," he said, after a moment, and made a little bow. "And which of the Misses Denham have I the honour of addressing?"

"Oh, I am Catherine. Gerard," she said, thoughtfully repeating the name. "I can't say that I remember ever hearing —"

"Possibly not. I'm afraid it's some years since I last met any member of your family — so long ago, in fact, that you must still have been in the schoolroom. However, both your father and myself are members of White's and have several acquaintances in common. One of them you mentioned just now — Viscount Pamyngton."

She looked a little shamefaced. "Yes, well, perhaps you ought to forget about that," she mumbled. "I was so distracted, thinking I could never make anyone believe the truth of my story — what is he like?"

"I beg your pardon?" Clearly, he was puzzled by the question.

"My Lord Pamyngton, I mean. What kind of man is he?"

"Hard to say," he replied, with a shrug. "Much like any other fellow, I suppose."

She tossed her long hair back with an impatient gesture.

"But he must have *some* distinguishing features — either of countenance or of character!" she insisted.

"Not at all. I assure you he is far from being distinguished in any way."

She frowned. "You don't seem to think much of him."

"Perhaps I know him too well. But I assure you that I have his interests at heart, all the same. That's why I would like to know what he can possibly have done to incur your hatred."

"Well, I dare say I may tell you on my way back home. After all, if you're willing to help me, I suppose I owe you some explanation of my present predicament. Oh, how I wish that I could fasten up my hair again!" she exclaimed, impatiently, twisting it into a coil. "But it's no use — I lost the pins when I was fighting off that horrible creature!"

"No doubt I could persuade the good woman of the inn to provide some for you."

"Oh, but she is so disagreeable! I don't think I could face her again."

"Then by all means let us leave things as they are. If I may say so, it is a prodigiously becoming hair style."

"Do you really think so?" The demure face was quickly transformed by a saucy smile. If she had turned that look upon the man she met by the roadside, thought Gerard, she had only herself to blame for what had followed. What on earth had she been doing, anyway, wandering about unescorted and without money? No doubt if he were patient he might learn this presently, along with the details of Pamyngton's offence.

"Indeed I do. But we'd best be on our way, for it will be dark presently. Have you any baggage to collect?"

"Yes, I did have a small portmanteau. I think it was put down in the hall, before —" she shivered — "before there was all the trouble."

He nodded and opened the door for her to pass into the hall. He followed, picking up the bag which was standing at the foot of the staircase.

"Is this the one?"

"Yes, that's mine."

"I suppose, ma'am, it doesn't by any chance contain a wrap? If so, I should recommend you to wear it."

She thanked him, and, after rummaging in the bag, produced a fine shawl which he helped her to place around her shoulders. This operation had just been completed when the landlord came out of the back quarters, followed in a few moments by his wife.

"So you're off, then," said the woman, with a sniff. "Decided not to wait for your gentleman friend with the doctor, I see."

Gerard drew away from Miss Denham and, producing his purse, placed a gold sovereign in the innkeeper's ready hand.

"I doubt if you'll ever see that person here again, with or without a doctor, my good woman. And I would be obliged if you would contrive to forget, too, that you ever saw this young lady in his company."

"Why, to be sure, y'r honour!"

Bowing, the innkeeper watched them as they walked across the cobbled yard. The gentleman tossed the luggage to his tiger and then handed the young lady up into the curricle before mounting himself and taking up the reins.

"Nice goings on!" commented the landlord to his wife. "She's a rare baggage, that miss, I'll warrant, getting herself two men in the space o' half an hour! Still, it's human nature, I s'pose, and we've not done so badly out o' it."

Chapter II: Viscount Pamyngton's Offence

By now the sun had sunk below the horizon, and dark purple masses of cloud were obscuring the red and gold of the sky.

The girl sat silent, while the gentleman gave all his attention to the road for a time. Presently she roused herself and asked, "Do you know the way, Mr. Gerard, or should I direct you?"

"I believe you may safely leave it to me. We keep to this road until we are about two miles short of Cowfold, then turn left. Isn't that so?"

"Yes." She sighed, with a mixture of relief and fatigue. "I can't tell you how thankful I am to be going home — and I will never, never try to run away again!"

He glanced at her sharply. "That is what you were doing?"

She nodded. "Yes, I was. Oh, it seems rather stupid now, but at the time I thought it a good idea."

He hesitated for a moment. "I've no wish to pry into your concerns," he said, diffidently, "but may I be allowed to know why you were running away?"

"Of course, for I do owe you some explanation. Only it is rather a complicated matter to explain. You see, I have a married sister who lives in Brighton."

She paused for a few moments; he waited hopefully, then ventured to prompt her.

"And the possession of a married sister in Brighton has this unfortunate effect upon you, I collect. Do you run away often, ma'am?"

She gave a little gurgle of laughter. "How absurd you are! No, of course not. But the thing was, that we — my two sisters and I — were to go down tomorrow to stay with Fanny for the start of the Brighton races. We were so looking forward to it! At least," she added, with a characteristic liking for accuracy, "Nell and I were in transports, but Louisa was not so well pleased. She — she has her reasons, but that's beside the point. Anyway, something happened, and Mama said that we might not go until — until —" her voice wavered — "oh, perhaps not at all this season!" she finished indignantly.

"And so you decided to flout your parents' wishes, and go alone?"

She flashed a warm smile at him. "You are very quick, sir," she approved. "Yes, I did. I don't usually disobey my parents — it's not worth while, for they are quite strict — but this didn't seem so very dreadful. I was only going to my own sister, after all," she said, with a defiance that was evidently meant to convince herself, "and I know Fanny would have stood up for me. In any case, we were being done out of our treat for such a stupid reason!"

He was naturally curious to know what the reason was, but it did not seem as though she meant to enlighten him. After another short pause, she continued the story at a different point.

"They were all going to dine at my uncle's house this evening. I pleaded the headache — indeed, I had one, truly, after disputing so much with Mama after Lady N—" She pulled herself up short and looked at him in a guilty way. "After the letter came," she finished, a trifle weakly.

"The letter?"

"It was a letter Mama received this morning that made her say we could no longer go to Brighton. Anyway, I said I didn't wish to go with them to my uncle's, and they were quite content to leave me on my own. Mama said I would get over my sulks best if they let me alone," she finished, with a pout.

"Even the best of mothers can be unfeeling at times," he agreed. "So when they had gone, you packed your bag and prepared to leave for Brighton. I imagine you would have left a note to explain where you intended to go?"

She nodded. "With any luck, we should arrive home hours before they do, and I can tear it up."

"So you've decided against making another attempt to run away to Brighton?" he asked, in a teasing tone.

"Indeed I have! This one was quite enough for me. Nell says I am no good at concocting schemes, and I begin to think she is right, for absolutely everything that could go wrong with this one, did. First of all, there was Stella."

"Stella?"

"She's Nell's pony. She's very good with Nell, but not with anyone else, and in any case, I am no horsewoman. You may as well know that from the start."

"In case I am ever tempted to invite you to ride with me?" he murmured.

She laughed again, a pleasant, relaxed sound that brought an answering smile to his face.

"I assure you, it would not be a success. I had far rather drive with you."

He looked round at her, noticing for the first time the unusual colour of her eyes, a colour that reminded him of nothing so much as a glass of rich, golden sherry wine.

"May I hold you to that promise?" he asked, quietly.

She was taken aback for a moment. "Oh — well — I am driving with you now," she said, hastily. "But — let me finish what I was telling you, for I don't doubt you will find it vastly diverting. I took Stella because she was the only animal I could get at without the grooms noticing. Of course, it was a mistake," she added, bitterly. "The wretched creature wouldn't let me tie my baggage on, so I had to place it before me on the saddle. Then no sooner did we get out on to the road than she started to play off her tricks on me. I managed to keep her going for a few miles, but soon the portmanteau rolled off, and when I dismounted to recover it, she took to her heels and went back home."

"How do you know she returned home?"

"Oh, she always does, whenever I come off her! Depend on it, she'll be safe in the stable when we reach the house."

"Had you planned to ride this frisky beast all the way to Brighton, Miss Denham? Surely that was a little optimistic?" he asked, with a smile.

"Oh, no. I am not quite so stupid as that! I meant to ride to Cuckfield, then take the stage coach."

He raised his eyebrows. "The stage coach! That was — enterprising — of you."

"Well, I know it isn't the thing for a female to travel by stage coach, but I really had no choice. I couldn't use the family carriage, and I hadn't enough money by me to pay for a post chaise. In any case," she went on, a little crestfallen, "I forgot to put the money in my reticule in all the flurry of getting away, though I didn't discover that until later."

"Oh, dear," he said sympathetically, "I fear you are not very expert in this business of running away."

"If you knew me well," said Catherine Denham despondently, "you would know that I'm not really very expert in anything."

"Come," he said, in a rallying tone, "you are still suffering from a natural chagrin at the failure of your scheme. Just now you will be more in charity with yourself, and ready to admit that you have the usual number of accomplishments laid claim to by every young lady."

"Well," she admitted, grudgingly, "I am not so bad at some things, perhaps. Anything of an artistic nature — but that is little to the purpose when one is trying to keep one's seat on a skittish creature like Stella! I tell you, I had far rather have been a famous horsewoman at that moment than almost anything else in the world!"

He nodded sympathetically. "So what did you do after your horse took to its heels?"

"I thought I would walk the rest of the way. I'd left home in plenty of time, and had less than four miles still to cover. Four miles," she said, with a rueful laugh, "does not sound very much, at the start of a journey. But by the time I had done half of it, I began to think it was not such a very good notion to run away, after all. The road was so rough and dusty, and my shoes seemed painfully thin and the bag unbearably heavy —! However, I was not going to give in, because I now had farther to go back home than to go forward. I trudged on, and reached Cuckfield at last, only to find that the stage coach had left half an hour previously! I could have wept," she declared, tragically, "but that it wouldn't have done the slightest good."

"It was certainly very hard on you," he said, sympathetically, "after so much valiant effort. So what did you do then, ma'am?"

"Well, then," she replied with a laugh, "I made the unwelcome discovery that I'd come out without any money. I spent ages trying to persuade the landlord of the inn to hire me a chaise that would be paid for at my destination. I almost succeeded, too, for he was quite a sympathetic man; but his wife wouldn't hear of it." She sighed. "I always find men are much easier to persuade into anything than females."

He smiled. "I dare say you might. So I suppose there was nothing for you to do but start to walk back home again?"

"I couldn't think of anything else," she admitted, "though I dreaded the prospect. That was why I was so foolish as to accept a lift from that — that abominable person! Of course, it was most improper, I realized that —"

"But you were scarcely in a situation to consider the proprieties," he suggested.

"No. And he did seem very respectful, at first. But then he stopped at the inn we've just left, saying he must have some refreshment. He constrained me to get down, though I assured him I wanted nothing but to reach home as quickly as possible. And then — and then —" her voice faltered, and died.

"I know the rest," he said quickly. "Pray don't distress yourself by dwelling on it. My only regret is that I never set eyes on this — gentleman — myself. But at the time I thought there was some kind of tipsy brawl going on, and my only concern was to avoid it. It wasn't until I heard you mention your name —"

"What a mercy that you were there, and knew my family! I can't think what I would have done next, even if, as you suggested, that dreadful man had really no intention of returning. I don't think," she finished, doubtfully, "that I should have had any more success in persuading the innkeeper there to help me than I did with the one at Cuckfield."

"Perhaps not; but you needn't think of the disagreeable affair any more. There is one thing I would like to know, though, if you feel disposed to enlighten me."

"At the moment, I am so grateful for your help I feel disposed to tell you anything. What is it you wish to know, sir?"

"Only the part played by Pamyngton in this affair," he said, after a slight hesitation.

"Oh!" She glanced at him quickly and was silent for a moment.

"If you would rather not, of course —"

"It's only that he's a friend of yours, and I have no wish to embarrass you," she replied quickly.

"What on earth can the wretched fellow have been up to?" he asked, turning a dismayed look on her.

She laughed. "It's not so very bad — indeed it's not really his fault at all. You see, the thing is — perhaps you may know this already — that my Lord Pamyngton is looking about him for a wife."

The horses swerved suddenly, and for a few moments Mr. Gerard gave his attention to setting them right.

"Careless of me," he said, presently. "Really, Miss Denham, I find your information most interesting. I myself had no idea of it, I assure you."

"Hadn't you? Well, at any rate, it must be true, for we have it from his mother, the Countess of Nevern, who is a very old friend of my Mama's."

"It is truly most creditable, the way in which mothers busy themselves with their offspring's most intimate concerns," he remarked dryly.

"Yes, I know what you mean. Females expect it, of course, but it must be vastly disagreeable to a gentleman. But, all the same, I believe Lord Pamyngton must indeed be thinking of marriage, for he is the only son, is he not, and almost thirty years of age?"

"True," he answered, curtly. "But I don't quite see why any such notions of his could possibly affect your plans for a visit to Brighton."

She looked at him in some embarrassment. "That isn't quite so easy to explain," she said, slowly. "You see, it was like this.

Mama received a letter from Lady Nevern saying that her son was staying with his parents at Nevern Hall for a few weeks, and inviting all of us to dine there tomorrow. And — and she said that he was — was thinking of marriage, and where better could he look than among the family of her dearest friend — that meant Mama, of course," she explained, hurriedly.

He nodded, but made no reply. Out of the corner of her eye, she saw that his mouth had taken on a stern look. She wondered if she had offended him by speaking of the personal affairs of one of his close friends, and fell silent.

"I collect that your mother concurred with this view?" he asked presently. "And that was why she insisted that the visit to your sister should be postponed?"

Miss Denham nodded. "Of course, you must realize, Mr. Gerard, that Mama has five daughters still to establish in the world," she replied, a little on the defensive. "Apart from that, she and Lady Nevern have always wanted a match between Viscount Pamyngton and one of us. You may, perhaps, have heard that at one time it was to be my eldest sister, Frances. Nothing came of that, however."

He nodded, keeping his eyes on the road.

"Of course, Lord Pamyngton didn't precisely *jilt* Fanny," continued Catherine, reflectively, "for nothing was settled between them in an official way, so to speak. But I do remember hearing that it was a great disappointment to both families when he fell madly in love with someone else. I wasn't supposed to know anything about these matters, though," she concluded, turning to him with an impish smile, "because I was only a schoolgirl of fourteen at the time. It's surprising how much one does manage to hear, I must say, even in the sheltered precincts of the schoolroom!"

He made no answer for a moment, then said abruptly, "As you remark, that all happened long ago."

"Yes, more than five years since. I never saw the lady in the case, any more than I did Lord Pamyngton, but I was told that she was ravishingly lovely — they called her the Toast of the Town. Pray, sir, did you ever meet Georgiana Eversley, as she was then?"

Twilight had gathered about them, and she could no longer see the expression on his face clearly; but there seemed to be some constraint in his voice as he answered her.

"Yes, I was acquainted with her. As you say, she was — very lovely."

"He would have done better to have taken Fanny, though," remarked Catherine, wisely, "for Miss Eversley married someone else in the end. But I'm glad he didn't, for I like Fanny's husband, Colonel Hailsham, prodigiously. And I'm not at all sure that I should like Viscount Pamyngton — if you'll forgive my saying such a thing of a friend of yours!"

"How has he incurred your displeasure? By depriving you of the visit to Brighton, even if inadvertently? Or is there anything else that you hold against him?"

"W-ell," she replied, drawing the word out while she thought this question over, "perhaps not — though I have an uneasy feeling — oh, dear, it is rather difficult to tell you."

"Perhaps I should not ask."

She studied him thoughtfully. They had just come to the point at which they left the main road for a side turning, and she watched as he skilfully guided the horses round the bend into the narrow, winding lane which led eventually to Eastridge House.

"The thing is, you see," she said, emboldened by the fact that his attention was not wholly upon her, "that I have a strong notion Mama thinks I am the most likely candidate for his favour. Not that I am the best looking of the three — far from it — Louisa is the handsomest, and Nell the most attractive. But the trouble is that Louisa is not precisely in either looks or spirits at present. Poor Lou," she added, compassionately, "she's fallen in love with someone quite unsuitable, and I fear Mama will never relent towards him. And, of course, Nell is younger than I am, so naturally Mama will think first of my claims to notice."

"So it is to be all settled without reference to my friend Pamyngton?" he asked, with a dry little laugh.

"Oh dear! I fear I have vexed you," she said, looking doubtfully at him. "Perhaps we had better not speak of it any more."

"Not at all. I am merely amused to have this insight into the workings of the female mind."

"You *are* vexed!" she exclaimed, in dismay. "I am so sorry. I should have held my tongue — Mama often tells me that I allow it to run away with me."

"Let me assure you, ma'am, that I would not have missed your revelations for a good deal," he replied, smiling into her eyes for a moment with restored good humour. "I find your conversation most refreshing, and of far more interest than if we had merely passed the time in talking of the weather, or some such socially acceptable topic."

"No, do you really? I expect," she added sensibly, "you are just saying that to be kind, but I don't care, for it is vastly pleasing!"

"Will you carry your candour a little further?" he asked. "Will you tell me honestly what your answer would be if it chanced that Pamyngton should come seeking your hand?"

"Readily," answered Catherine, with a light laugh. "I do not wish for the honour of his addresses."

"Although you have never met him?"

"Meeting him could make no difference to my feelings."

"You are severe," he said, mockingly. "Is this all because of your disappointment over Brighton?"

"No, not at all."

"What, then?"

"Because," replied Catherine, warmly, "I have no wish to be a second-best bride."

"Second-best? I don't quite see —"

"We know, don't we, that he was head over heels in love with Georgiana Eversley? So if he wants to wed now, it would be simply a marriage of convenience. And that," she finished, decidedly, "would not be good enough for me!"

He looked at her again. The twilight had deepened, and her face showed palely in the gloom, the eyes darkened and mysterious.

"You would prefer a love match?" he asked, quietly.

"Indeed I should. If I ever marry, Mr. Gerard, it will be because I find myself unable to live without — whoever it is! And he must love me to distraction," she went on, with an expressive gesture of her hands, "and load me with jewels and gee-gaws, and send me flowers every day — but only those that are out of season — and — oh, all manner of absurd and extravagant things! But it is quite certain that I wouldn't want anyone who was languishing with love for some other female, and only offered for me because he wished for a marriage of convenience!"

A short silence followed this outburst.

"I see," he said, at last. "Yes, I think you are very wise. With all your charm and beauty — if you will allow me to say so — you have the right to expect nothing less."

"Why, so I think, though you are kind enough to flatter me beyond my desserts. No one has ever called me *wise*, before, precisely, though Grandmama says that my head's screwed on the right way, in spite of my nonsense."

"I am sure she is right. Well, then, Miss Denham, I fear there can be no hope for my friend Pamyngton finding an alliance in your family, and he may just as well tell your mother to permit you to go to Brighton."

She laughed. "I should like to see that! But his case is not quite hopeless — Nell says she will have him, if he asks her, no matter how disagreeable he may be, because she would dearly love to be the wife of a Viscount!" She sobered a little. "But I ought not to have told you that, for it was just our fun, you know, and Nell didn't really mean it — at least," she added, thoughtfully, "I don't think she did."

He changed the subject at this point by asking her which turning to take next. She set him right, and soon they arrived at the iron gates of Eastridge House. He was about to turn the equipage into the short drive which led to the house, but she leaned over, touching his arm.

"No, please do not drive me up to the door, for the servants will see us, and Mama is sure to hear of it. I will go quietly round to the side entrance. It's never locked until much later than this, and I can contrive to slip in without anyone noticing."

"As you wish, ma'am."

He jumped down, summoning the boy Jack to take charge of the horses. Then he assisted Miss Denham to alight and, picking up her portmanteau, offered her his free arm. She hung back.

"But I do not need you to come with me, sir," she protested. "Indeed, I am more likely to escape notice if I go alone."

"You will not wish to carry this wretched bag any further this evening, I should imagine? Besides, I should prefer to see you safely indoors before I leave you."

She yielded to his persuasions. "Very well, then, if you must. But I think we had better walk in the shadow of the trees, for I see that the curtains are not yet drawn, and someone may chance to see us."

He thought it unlikely that anyone would notice them approach in the fast-gathering darkness, but did not trouble to say so.

They went through the gate, and together walked in the shelter of the trees which bordered the drive until they reached the house. She had nothing to say, evidently occupied with her thoughts; and he did not break the silence.

Only when they reached the side entrance did she speak, turning towards him and holding out her hand.

"I can find no adequate words for thanking you, Mr. Gerard — you have been a friend indeed! I only wish I may not have brought you too far out of your way."

He took her hand and bowed over it. "I beg you won't mention it, Miss Denham. I have found it a most — intriguing — experience."

She accepted the portmanteau from him, and turned towards the door.

"Possibly we may meet again some time," she whispered. "Once again, my most sincere thanks."

"I think perhaps we may. Meantime, may I beg you not to think too hardly of my poor friend Pamyngton?"

"I have almost forgiven him," she replied, in a low voice, as she softly opened the door and slipped inside, out of his sight.

Chapter III: Eleanor is Curious

Catherine Denham arrived late at the breakfast table on the morning following her escapade. Her two youngest sisters had finished and were following their governess to the schoolroom; her father, she noticed with relief, had already gone about his own concerns.

"So you have condescended to put in an appearance at last, miss," remarked her mother, sarcastically. "It's to be hoped you have benefited from your long sleep, and are in a better humour than when we parted yesterday."

"Yes, thank you, Mama," replied Catherine meekly.

"Is your headache quite gone?" asked Louisa, in a kind tone, as she passed the bread and butter.

"A headache of *that* kind," stated Lady Denham, "troubles no one for long."

"Well, it did get better quite soon," admitted Catherine. "May I have some fresh tea, Mama?"

Lady Denham signalled to Eleanor to ring the bell, as she was nearest to it.

"What did you do with yourself, Katie?" asked Eleanor as she obeyed.

"Oh, this and that," replied Catherine, with a shrug. "I finished reading Maria Edgeworth's 'Belinda' for one thing, so you may have it now, Lou."

"That's not fair!" exclaimed Eleanor, hotly. "You know it was my turn to have it next!"

"I'd forgotten. Anyway, it doesn't matter, for I don't think you'll like it as well as 'Castle Rackrent'. I didn't."

"What a pity! Still, it will do to tide me over until the next lot of novels arrive from the Circulating library, I dare say."

"Really, one would suppose to listen to you girls that your home offered no rational occupations such as music, needlework or conversation," said Lady Denham tartly. "You spend far too much of your time reading novels. They are unwholesome, and vastly lowering to one's moral tone. I'm sure there is an abundance of good reading on your father's bookshelves, without your needing to rely on the services of the Circulating library."

"True, Mama," replied Catherine. "But I do think we've read most of the books there which are likely to interest us."

"It would do you a deal of good to try some of those which you don't believe you would find interesting. One must sometimes think of improving the mind. There are some very fine volumes of sermons —"

Groans greeted this remark. She laughed suddenly, changing her tone.

"Well, I must confess they are not the reading I myself would have chosen at your age. Since you are determined to be frivolous, tell me what you've decided to wear at Nevern Hall this evening. Naturally, I am anxious that you should all look your best."

"But if we all look our best," protested Catherine, with a saucy smile, "then my Lord Pamyngton may offer for all three of us, and the fat would be in the fire!"

"I'll be satisfied if he offers for one of you. It ought to be you, my dear," said Lady Denham, turning to Louisa. "You are the eldest — and the handsomest."

"I — I don't aspire to it, Mama," stammered Louisa, looking upset.

"No. I am very well aware that you do not," replied her mother, in a vexed tone. "I am also aware of your reason. And I tell you, Louisa, that if you do not have done with this nonsense I shall pack you off for a twelvemonth to your Great Aunt Maria in Cheltenham. You are one and twenty, and practically on the shelf, all due to your own folly! It will not do, miss — it will not do at all — and if you can't see where your own interest lies, you must be made to, that is all!"

"I mean to wear my new pink spotted muslin," put in Eleanor, with the worthy object of drawing her mother's attention away from Louisa, whose lip was trembling, "If we are not to go to Brighton this season, there is no point in hiding it away. And I promise you that if Viscount Pamyngton should offer for me, I would accept him at once! I should dearly love to be a Countess one day, and mistress of Nevern Hall, which is by far the handsomest residence hereabouts!"

"Yes, I dare say you would, child, and I am very pleased to hear it," replied her mother, somewhat mollified. "But after Louisa, Catherine has the first claim."

"Oh, you can leave me out of it," said Catherine, with a grimace. "I have no wish to be any man's second choice."

"What do you mean?" asked her mother, sharply.

"Only that everyone knows Viscount Pamyngton was madly in love with that Eversley female all those years ago. If he thinks of marriage now, it is only a matter of convenience."

"What stupid romantic notions have you got in your head now?" demanded Lady Denham, contemptuously. "It all comes of this novel-reading! What if he did happen to be head over heels in love with Georgiana Eversley that was? A man is not going to wear the willow for all those years, you may depend! By now he will be more than ready to place his affections elsewhere, as you would readily understand if you knew more of gentlemen and their ways."

"All the same," replied Catherine, stubbornly, "I don't think of marrying and settling down at all at present. I want to attend a great many more balls and parties, and meet many other eligible gentlemen —"

"Then you are very stupid, let me tell you! An advantageous match doesn't present itself so often that a girl can afford to let a chance slip, not even when she is fortunate enough, as you are, to be both attractive and well-dowered," stated Lady Denham, firmly. "You may have dozens of offers without there being one that comes near this! Upon my word," she added, working herself up into a state of vexation, "it is hard on a woman who still has five daughters to establish creditably in the world, and who finds them so blind to their own interest!"

They thought it best not to reply to this outburst, and for a while the room was silent.

"Katie," remarked Eleanor, after an interval, "what on earth have you been doing to your new gown, the aquamarine one that you meant to take to Fanny's? I saw Fincher coming out of your room with it over her arm earlier on, and it was dreadfully creased, just as though you had slept in it."

"Oh, did you?" asked Catherine, looking uneasily at her mother, who was rising from the table. "Well, the thing is I started to do some packing before I knew that we were not to go to Brighton."

"Packing is best left to your maid, who understands how it should be done," said Lady Denham, as she moved to the door. "Still, it is just what I should expect — another instance of your stupidity!"

She swept out of the room in a huff, and the girls eyed each other uneasily.

"She's in a fine pet," said Catherine. "Unless someone comes to call this morning, she will be out of humour all day, you may depend!"

"Let's escape it by walking down to the village," suggested Eleanor. "I want to try and find some pink ribbon to match my gown, and it's a lovely morning. A breath of fresh air will do us all good."

When she considered the matter, Catherine admitted that she had one or two purchases to make as well, and soon they were all strolling along the road that led to Holm Green.

"It's too hot for riding, or I might have been tempted to take Stella out," remarked Eleanor, as they passed the entrance to the stables of Eastridge House. "That reminds me, Katie — did you take Stella out yesterday evening, by any chance?"

"Why on earth should you ask?" replied her sister, with elaborate unconcern.

"Because I saw Biggs earlier on, and he told me that he found Stella wandering about the yard, ready saddled, just before we returned home yesterday evening. There was no one but you at home at that time, so naturally I thought you must be the culprit."

"Upon my word, you've been very busy this morning!" exclaimed Catherine, with a forced laugh. "Whatever time did you get up, pray?"

"Earlier than you, at any rate. And don't think to fob me off. Admit now, it was you who saddled my pony, wasn't it?"

"Well, yes, it was. I thought a ride might blow away my headache."

Eleanor laughed unkindly. "More likely to give you one, considering how badly you manage Stella!"

"She's a pesky beast, and I detest her! The worst of it is, I think the feeling's reciprocated."

"Well, I'll thank you not to take my pony again. You had no right, without asking me."

"But you weren't there to ask — and, anyway, I did the silly creature no harm."

"How far did you take her, then?" demanded Eleanor, suspiciously.

Louisa intervened at this point. "Really, if you two mean to squabble all the time, I shall begin to wish I had stayed at home. Can't you find some other subject of conversation?"

"I am only too willing to do so," said Catherine, virtuously. "*I* didn't choose this one."

Eleanor directed a searching glance at her. "You know what, Katie, I think you've been up to something. What it is, I don't know, but I'll find out, never fear!"

"I am all a-tremble at the prospect," said Catherine, derisively.

"I am more concerned about Mama's pre-occupation with the prospects of a match between Viscount Pamyngton and one of us," remarked Louisa, in a troubled tone. "For one thing, it will be so very awkward to meet him this evening knowing that such a thought is in the minds of nearly everyone present. It doesn't make for easy, natural conversation."

"Then let us state our position immediately!" laughed Catherine. She sketched a curtsy. "My Lord, we are delighted to make your acquaintance, but wish to say at once that we haven't the faintest desire to wed you. At least," she added, her eyes dancing, "my sister Nell wouldn't mind so much, provided you could arrange to get rid of your parents as soon as possible and make her a Countess, and mistress of Nevern Hall!"

"Katie, you clown!" exclaimed Eleanor, breaking into laughter.

Even Louisa's gravity was shaken, and all three were laughing heartily when they heard a carriage approaching. They just had time to stand close in to the hedge, still doubled up with mirth, before a curricle drove past them.

As it was approaching, the gentleman in the driving seat gave them a casual glance which soon hardened into a frank stare. When he drew level to pass, he touched his hat and bowed.

They stood looking after him until the vehicle had disappeared round the next bend.

"Well!" exclaimed Louisa. "For the life of me, I do not know who that was!"

"Nor I," agreed Eleanor. She turned to Catherine. "But I'll wager you do, Katie! It was you he looked at particularly! Who is he, and where have you met him before?"

"Nonsense!" replied Catherine, airily. "How can you say so? He looked at all of us, and no wonder, for we were making fine exhibitions of ourselves, laughing fit to die!"

"Well, he did acknowledge one of us — or all of us," said Louisa, thoughtfully. "Of course, he may just have been exercising misplaced gallantry, seeing three females on the road unescorted, and in a most improper state of mirth."

"I don't believe that — it was Katie he bowed to," persisted Eleanor. "And I think she knows it was, too — see, she is blushing, now, I do declare!"

Catherine was annoyed to find that this was true. She wished, not for the first time, that her younger sister did not have such keen powers of observation, and set about putting her off the scent.

"What nonsense you talk, Nell! I'm sure the weather is warm enough to give anyone a touch of colour! But if you insist on making a drama of it, why, yes, I will confess all!" She threw out her arms in an extravagant gesture. "He is my lover!" she whispered, dramatically. "Last night, when you were all asleep in your beds, I crept out and met him by moonlight! Was there a moon? I forget — anyway, it doesn't matter, for it's always moonlight when lovers meet! We planned to elope, but I could only manage things by riding Stella all the way to Gretna Green —"

She had succeeded. Neither of her sisters could stop laughing for long enough to press any sensible questions on her; and by the time they sobered again, they had reached the village, and the incident was put aside for the moment.

Presently something occurred which drove it from their minds altogether.

Chapter IV: Star-crossed Lovers

They had passed the first group of cottages and were walking beside the wall of the churchyard when a gentleman came through the lynch gate and turned to walk in their direction. He was a dark, good-looking young man, but the expression on his face matched the sober hue of the suit he was wearing. As they came face to face he halted, hesitated for a moment as though taken unawares, then raised his hat and bowed. The girls, too, paused uncertainly; then Catherine and Eleanor said good morning.

He answered them gravely and stood still, his eyes on Louisa, who neither moved nor spoke.

"We were just walking along to Mrs. Lippitt's shop to make some purchases," said Catherine, breaking the awkward silence. "It — it is such a fine morning, is it not? Far too pleasant to waste indoors!"

He agreed, but without much conviction. "I must not detain you," he added. "It is fortunate that we should have met, for it enables me to bid you good-bye. I am going away from home tomorrow and expect to be absent for some time."

"Going away?" Louisa whispered, raising her head at these words and showing the distress in her face.

"Yes, Miss Denham. I have taken a post as tutor for a time in another part of the country."

There was another silence. The young man continued to look steadily at Louisa, who would not meet his eyes. It was evident that both of them had almost forgotten the presence of the two younger girls.

"I am sure you will wish to tell Lou all about it," exclaimed Catherine, tugging at Eleanor's gown, surreptitiously. "And as she has no purchases to make, perhaps we may leave her in your charge for a little while. I should think," she added, with some forethought, "it might be cooler walking in the churchyard, besides being more private. Come along, Nell."

She seized her younger sister's arm and was about to hustle her away when Louisa put out an unsteady hand to stop them.

"Don't go, Katie!" she said, in a tremulous voice. "I must not — you know I promised —"

"We shall be back in a few moments," insisted Catherine; then, in a lower tone which could only reach her sister's ear — "You cannot leave him without even saying goodbye! Go with him, love, and for once never mind about Mama!"

Louisa shook her head, but did not try to detain them any more. She watched them walk away, then turned to the young man, who was still studying her in silence.

"I should not," she said, shakily. "You know I should not! I promised my parents — we both did! — that we would not write to each other or try to — to meet again!"

"We have kept that promise," he said, firmly. "This is a chance meeting, but I think it right that we should speak together once more before we part for good. There are things which need to be said between us. When last we met, we were both too overcome by your parents' refusal of my application for your hand in marriage, even though it was expected. I could not think clearly — I needed time for reflection."

"What good can it do?" she asked, despondently. "Nothing can alter their decision, and I am bound to obey them."

"I would not wish to deny that you have a duty to your parents. But don't forget that you also have a duty to yourself, Louisa. You are not a child — you are one and twenty, and therefore of an age to have some say in what concerns you so nearly."

"You think I should defy them, Oliver?" she asked, incredulously. "No, you couldn't say that — you, a clergyman!"

He shook his head. "I don't say it. I am only thinking that should they try to push you into a loveless marriage with someone else, you would have the right to oppose them. Oh, my love!"

She caught her breath at the endearment.

"I will call you so," he said, sadly, "just for this little while that we can be together. It may be for the last time."

"Don't," she exclaimed, on a sob.

"No. I must try not to distress you, for we have so little time, and what I have to say is important." His voice became firmer now. "We both know, dearest, that the living to which I am soon to succeed will not, as your parents pointed out, enable me to keep you in the style to which you've been accustomed."

"As if I cared for that!" she cried, in a strangled tone. "I have fortune enough for us both!"

"But I must care for it, my dearest. What kind of a man can be content to live on his wife's fortune? Your parents are quite right to say that I must not take advantage of your present feelings for me, that you can make a more equal match —"

"Oh, Oliver!" She looked up at him, her eyes swimming in tears. "What do I care so long as we can be together? I would rather live in a hovel with you, than in a palace with any other man!"

"So you think now."

She stared at him, aghast. "You don't believe me? You think — dear God, what can you mean?"

"If you look at me like that," he said, smiling wryly, "I shan't have the remotest chance of telling you what I mean. But we have so little time, my dearest — I must try to keep a hold on myself. What I want to say is this. You must try to forget me."

"Forget you?" she repeated, weakly. "Oh, Oliver — my dearest — do you think that I could?"

"I don't wish to think it," he answered, grimly, "but we both of us know such changes do occur. Have you no female friends who have thought themselves deep in love with a certain man at one time, and then six months later have been just as decided in their preference for another? I have seen this happen to many of my own friends."

A little colour came into Louisa's cheeks, and she raised her chin. "So you believe that what we feel for each other is no more than a mere infatuation?" she asked, in a challenging tone.

His lips set in a firm line. "It is safer not to ask what I believe," he said, with some constraint. "What I am proposing is that we should put our feelings for each other to the test. As I told you, I am going away until the living which has been promised to me falls vacant. That will be almost a year hence. We shall never meet by chance, as we must have done had I stayed here; and we have promised not to correspond with each other. We shall therefore be completely cut off during that time. It is a lengthy period —" his voice wavered for a second, but recovered immediately — "long enough for us to discover the truth. If at the end of it, we still feel the same as we do today —"

"Oh, I know that *I* shall!" breathed Louisa.

"If so, then we must make a stand with your parents," he finished, firmly. "We shall have the right to do so, then; the proof that our affections have endured not only the long separation, but all our determination to overcome them."

She looked at him doubtfully at these last words.

"That is what I meant when I said that you must try to forget me, Louisa," he said steadfastly. "There is only one way we can be sure that ours is indeed a love that means more to us than all other considerations. We must try — honestly and conscientiously — to overcome it."

A rush of tears blinded her, and she shook her head dumbly.

"Have you tried — really tried — to forget me, so far?" he demanded, steeling himself not to take her in his arms. "Have you exerted yourself to put all thoughts of me away from you, and to join in the amusements of your sisters?" He shook his head gently. "No, I see from your face that you haven't. Neither have I. But from the moment that we leave each other now, Louisa, we must do this very thing. It will be difficult —" His voice failed for a moment.

"Impossible!" sobbed Louisa.

"Not impossible — oh, do not cry, my love! I cannot bear it if you cry," he said, in a more natural tone that was charged with emotion.

They stood looking at each other for a moment in abject misery. A curl of hair had escaped from under her bonnet and lay against her cheek, dampened by tears. A little incoherent sound escaped him. He gathered her into his arms.

The bonnet fell back from her head, and he laid his lips against her golden hair. She clung to him, sobbing quietly.

After a time, he raised his head. "What have we done, to suffer so?" he said, harshly. "Our only fault is to love each other!"

The bitter words aroused Louisa's maternal feelings, never very far from the surface.

"Hush, my darling," she said, gently, stroking his face with soft fingers. "I have been selfish — forgive me! I must not make your task any harder than it is."

She disengaged herself, and found a handkerchief. Then she resolutely dried her eyes, and faced him with a brave smile.

"I promise," she said firmly. "I will try to do as you ask. I can see that you are right — that we must be quite sure —"

"It is not even as if I had any hopes of increasing my income as time goes on," he said, despondently. "As you know, one needs a patron for that — someone with a wealthy living in his gift, who would be willing to bestow it on me. And we have no family connection or close friends of the kind. I think, Louisa, the one thing I could not bear would be to see you regretting your choice after we had married, because of the difference in your circumstances! That is why I insist that we must be certain — certain that our affection is strong enough to withstand all our efforts to overcome it. Only so can we be sure that it will suffice to outweigh all the worldly advantages which you must forgo if we two marry."

She nodded. "You think we could persuade Mama and Papa to consent, if — if we do submit ourselves to this test?" she asked, doubtfully.

"If our love survives a year's separation, then it should be strong enough to conquer anything," he replied confidently. "Once *we* are sure, it will be easier to convince others. At present, I see the force of your parents' objections all too clearly. I have no right to persuade you into a disadvantageous marriage, without giving you time and opportunity to reflect." He paused, and looked into her face, his eyes deep and serious. "But you must make a strong effort to put all thoughts of me aside, Louisa, as I — God help me! — will do my best to overcome my feelings for you. Nothing else will constitute a true test. It may chance that you will succeed, and that someone else will take my place — I cannot flatter myself that there is any reason for you to attach yourself to me —"

"I can think of a dozen reasons," she interrupted, softly.

"But you will promise to try?"

"Yes," she answered, quietly. "I promise. It will not be easy—"

"There is help to be found, if you need it."

She nodded, too moved for speech. He took her hand and carried it to his lips, holding it there for a long time while he looked down at her as though he meant to imprint her image on his memory for ever.

They came back from a long distance to hear footsteps on the path leading up to the church, and saw that Louisa's sisters were already returning.

Chapter V: Dinner at Nevern Hall

The pillared portico of Nevern Hall glowed golden in the evening sunlight as the Denhams' carriage came sedately down the long avenue of trees which led to the house.

"There can be no doubt at all this is one of the handsomest residences hereabouts," remarked Lady Denham.

"Indeed, I agree with you, Mama!" exclaimed Eleanor. "The Etruscan room is beyond anything! Oh, why cannot we have a similar room in our house, Papa? I declare I would never sit anywhere else — I would stay there for ever!"

"Even that inducement fails to persuade me," replied her father, smiling. "I suppose some may care to have a whole room decorated with Wedgwood ware, but it isn't my taste. No, no; I prefer the small drawing-room, with its warm tapestries and comfortable wing chairs. A man can be at ease there, and not fancy he has strayed into some potter's showcase."

"It was designed by Robert Adam," said Lady Denham reproachfully.

"What has that to say to anything, my love? One either likes a thing, or one doesn't. I don't, and there's an end of the matter as far as I'm concerned."

"Papa, why don't we have some prodigious swell of an architect to renovate our house?" asked Catherine.

Her father eyed her severely. "Is that the kind of expression your mother permits you to use, young woman?"

"Indeed it is not!" snapped Lady Denham. "Catherine, you will mind your tongue in front of our hosts, or I shall have something to say to you afterwards. 'Prodigious swell', indeed! Where in the world did you pick up such a coarse expression?"

Eleanor was quick to rush to the rescue as her sister subsided, feeling crushed.

"No, but, Papa, why don't we make some improvements to the house?"

"What purpose would there be in it?" demanded Sir George. "I have no son to hand the place over to, and it suits your mother and myself well enough as it is. It might be different if we had an heir, but you girls will all marry and set up establishments of your own."

"I trust you may be right there, Denham," remarked his wife, dryly.

"Well, I know there are five of the chits still to see off," he replied, cheerfully, "but they're not too odiously ugly, and they're well provided for. I think we shall contrive to get rid of 'em all readily enough. At any rate," he concluded, with a wink at his daughters, "I'm determined to marry 'em off as soon as may be. Too much petticoat government in our household for my liking."

They all chided him for this remark, but it succeeded in restoring family good humour.

They were admitted to a spacious entrance hall decorated with classical sculptures set in niches, and conducted up a broad mahogany staircase to a room on the first floor. The two occupants of the room rose as soon as the visitors were announced and came forward hospitably to greet them.

"My dearest Sophie, how delightful to see you!"

The speaker was a somewhat plump lady in her fifties, with hair that was still golden and a face that bore traces of what had once been an exceptional beauty. There was a kindly expression round her mouth; but her blue eyes, though soft, were shrewd.

"It is an age since last we met!" went on Lady Nevern. "Far, far too long! And can this really be little Eleanor? Gracious, child, how you've grown! And Catherine, too — Louisa, of course, was full grown when last I saw her. But you are all so handsome — and so like your dear Mama! But there," she concluded, being blessed with a sensitivity which guarded her from the worst blunders of an incautious tongue, "young people do not care to hear such stuff, I know. Pray be seated. You will prefer the wing chair, Sir George, alongside Nevern, and you, Sophie, must join me on the sofa, so that we may enjoy a cosy little chat together." She broke off, turning to her husband. "You sent to inform James that our visitors are come, my dear?"

The Earl nodded, and continued with his task of seeing the young ladies comfortably settled. He was a tall, elegant man about five or six years older than the Countess, with brown hair greying at the temples, and dressed in the prevailing style. After everyone was seated, he dropped into a chair alongside Sir George Denham, and the two men were soon deep in conversation.

"We had an unexpected visitor today," remarked Lady Nevern, as she settled herself beside her friend on the sofa. "You'll recall the Eversleys, Sophie? That youngest son of theirs, Frederick, called in on his way down to Brighton to see James. He's going down for the Races, and is trying to persuade James to accompany him. Let us hope he will not succeed," she said, in a lower tone, sighing. "However, I have not seen Freddy Eversley since he was a schoolboy, and such a change as there is in him! He's now a fine, upstanding young man of four and twenty, with the Eversley hair and manner —

for all the world like that eldest brother of his, whom everyone called the Beau. You won't object to his making one of our party? He's staying here overnight."

Lady Denham had just begun to reassure her hostess on this point, for the inclusion of an eligible bachelor to the party could not be considered anything but an advantage, when the door opened to admit two gentlemen. One of them was obviously the young man whom Ariadne Nevern had that moment described; the second was some five years senior to Frederick Eversley, and bore such a marked resemblance to both the Earl and Countess that even those present who had never previously met him could have no difficulty in identifying him as Viscount Pamyngton.

To one person in the room, the realization came as a severe shock.

While the necessary introductions were being made, it suddenly occurred to Eleanor that her sister Catherine was behaving most oddly. At first, she stood stock still and stared, like any timid schoolgirl at her first social gathering. Louisa contrived to give her a gentle nudge so that she recovered sufficiently to make some response to the gentleman's bows; but afterwards she sank back into her chair and sat there without uttering a word, the most peculiar expression on her face.

Eleanor felt a lively curiosity at this conduct. It was unheard of for Katie to sit silent in company, and especially when there were young men present. On such occasions, she was the greatest rattle of them all. What could it mean? Even if Katie had not wished to come here this evening, and might still be feeling a trifle vexed at being denied the long anticipated trip to Brighton, Eleanor knew her sister well enough to be certain that she would have decided to make the best of things and derive what entertainment she could from the visit. It was her way, as it was Eleanor's, to take the present good and not to repine over the might have been.

She stole another look at her sister's face. What a very odd expression came over it whenever it was turned in Viscount Pamyngton's direction! What was it, exactly — shame, disgust, embarrassment? Something of all three, perhaps. But why? What could it mean?

Eleanor at last became conscious of the fact that Mr. Eversley, who had come to sit on her other side, was addressing some remark to her. She roused herself to answer him.

"I — I beg your pardon, sir? I fear I did not hear you perfectly."

"It's of no account, Miss Eleanor." There was a hint of laughter in his voice, as though he had noticed her abstraction. "Some inanity about the weather, merely, and you do very well to ignore it."

Eleanor flashed him a quick smile. "But we cannot afford to ignore the weather, sir," she said, with mock demureness. "Conversationally, where should we be without it? It's a tried and trusty friend, and I have been taught not to neglect old friends."

His green eyes twinkled. "Have you, indeed? That makes me wish that I might be included in their number. How long, now, do you suppose it might be, ma'am, before I could hope to qualify?"

"Oh, I have a friendly enough disposition, Mr. Eversley, in general; but an *old* friend — that is something it takes years to make," she answered, with a prim look which belied the sparkle in her eyes.

"It shall be my earnest endeavour from this day forward to earn the title. Only tell me how I may serve you, ma'am. Are there no dragons you wish slain, no treasures to be fetched back from far distant corners of the earth? Name the task, and it's as good as done, I assure you."

Her clear laugh rang out above the buzz of conversation in the room. "I see you are a humourist, sir. Katie," turning to the silent figure at her side, "here is Mr. Eversley offering to slay dragons on our behalf. Pray talk to him," she added, quickly, in an undertone, "for if you sit there quiet any longer, it will be remarked."

Catherine gave a little start, and coloured slightly; but the reproof succeeded in rousing her to take part in a light-hearted conversation with her sister and Frederick Eversley. Meanwhile Viscount Pamyngton was chatting with Sir George and Lady Denham, occasionally addressing a remark to Louisa, who was sitting near her parents.

Catherine's return to gaiety was short-lived. When the party presently adjourned to the dining-room, she found herself seated at table between her father and Viscount Pamyngton, with Eleanor and Frederick Eversley opposite. It was not so easy now to join in their conversation; and for a time her neighbour, Viscount Pamyngton, was engaged in talking to Louisa, who was seated on his other side.

Presently he turned towards Catherine, however, murmuring some polite enquiry about the dish she was being offered at the time. She answered him hurriedly, scarcely knowing what she said. He regarded her gravely, and after the footman had moved to serve those farther up the table, he said, softly, "Am I forgiven?"

"Forgiven? I — I don't quite know what you mean," she stammered.

"Come," he said, reproachfully, "surely you must. Or do you prefer to forget our previous meeting? If so, then of course I must defer to your decision. But I trust not — I ventured to hope that we might be friends."

"Friends!" she retorted, surprised into open indignation. "Well, sir, perhaps your friends do not choose to acknowledge their real names, but mine are very different, I assure you!"

"I deserve your scorn," he admitted, a rueful look in his deep blue eyes, so like those of Lady Nevern. "But it isn't quite as bad as you think, you know. Gerard *is* my name — one of my names, that is."

"A half lie is almost worse than a whole one," she answered, coldly.

"But what was I to do? You informed me straight away that you hated Pamyngton, and that the fault of your predicament lay at his door. I felt in honour bound to discover what I had done — all unconsciously — to harm you. It would have quite defeated this object had I admitted to you who I was. You would have told me nothing."

"That is what I find especially despicable," said Catherine, righteous anger for the moment overcoming her sense of the politeness due to a host. "By concealing your true identity, you — you *wormed* out of me all kinds of confidences which I should never have made, had I known who you really were! You cannot defend such conduct!"

"It was most reprehensible, I admit."

His tone was penitent enough, but she had a shrewd suspicion that he was in fact amused. This thought only served to increase her sense of injury.

"I suppose we may be thankful that at least you realize it," she replied, scornfully, turning her head away from him.

His eyes dwelt ruefully on the disdainful profile.

Frederick Eversley had not been able to catch Catherine's remark across the table, but he had noticed her cold tone and gesture towards his friend.

"Egad, you're never quarrelling with Pam, Miss Catherine?" he demanded, laughing. "You're to be congratulated — few people succeed in doing so. He's such a confounded smooth customer."

"Thank you, Freddy," drawled Pamyngton. "Be sure I shall come to your aid next time you may require a service of me."

"No, but truly you did sound vexed, Katie!" said Eleanor, gaily. She leaned across the table towards Pamyngton. "Did we not meet you on the road to the village this morning, sir? My sisters and I were out walking, and you were driving a curricle — I am almost certain it was you!"

"Yes, it was indeed, Miss Eleanor. I must apologize for not stopping, but I did not then have the pleasure of your acquaintance."

"Yes, but all the same, you recognized Katie, did you not, for you bowed to her?" persisted the irrepressible Eleanor. "And I can't imagine how in the world you two came to be acquainted!"

There was a moment's awkward silence.

"Surely one of the chief delights of imagination, Miss Eleanor," replied Pamyngton, lightly, "is that it can supply so many different solutions to every puzzle? You have only to exercise yours for a moment — for I'll warrant it is an uncommonly lively one — and I'll engage for it that you will at once think of a score of places where I may have been so fortunate as to chance to encounter your sister. The possibilities are limitless — I leave the choice to you."

He bowed slightly, and Frederick Eversley clapped his hands.

"Oh, well played, Pam!" he exclaimed, with a laugh. "Did you know, ladies, that he is a first-rate cricketer? Now you see what I meant when I called him a smooth customer, a while back. Make what you can of that answer, Miss Eleanor!"

Eleanor shrugged. "Oh, well of course, if it is such a secret —!"

"You talk a deal of nonsense, Nell!" exclaimed Catherine, tartly.

Frederick had sisters of his own, and saw trouble looming.

"Which of us does not?" he asked, smiling. "Here's Pam, for example — I ask him a straight question; will he accompany me to Brighton for the Races; and can I get a straight answer out of him? Nothing but a farrago of nonsense, I assure you, every time I broach the subject. However, I'm off tomorrow, and he must do the best he can without my company. I dare say, you know, he'll manage tolerably well, especially if you young ladies will take pity on him, and allow him to visit you now and then."

"I think you talk more nonsense than any of us, sir," laughed Eleanor, quite restored to her former good humour.

Pamyngton nodded. "Indeed, he does, Miss Eleanor. And I'll give you a straight answer now, Freddy, if you like. I've made up my mind to accompany you to Brighton tomorrow."

"You have? Capital! But why could you not say so at first, my dear fellow?"

"Put it down to my perverse nature."

This interchange was overheard by Lady Nevern, in the intervals of an animated conversation with her neighbour, Sir George Denham. A shadow crossed her face, and she tried to catch the eye of Lady Denham, who was sitting on Eleanor's other side. Failing in this, she ventured to voice a smiling protest.

"Perverse? You, James? Never! I am sure no one can have a more compliant nature. Oh, very well, I have done!" she finished, noticing the impatient look which momentarily crossed her son's face. "I know I must not praise you."

She turned to give her attention once more to Sir George, fervently hoping that she had managed to avoid showing her disappointment at this sudden change in her son's plans. But later, when dinner was over and the ladies were sitting alone in the drawing-room while the gentlemen lingered over their wine, she drew Sophia Denham aside.

"What are we to do, Sophie? Here's that wretched Eversley boy spoiling our little plan by persuading James to accompany him to Brighton! I must confess that William and I are disappointed on our own account for we had hoped to keep him at Nevern Hall for a few weeks, at any rate. However, when one's offspring are grown men and women —" she gave a little sigh — "one must be grateful for seeing them at all. You are more fortunate, my dear, in having six children, for you will never lack for the company of one or another."

"You would not think so," replied Sophia Denham, dryly, "if you had to look about you for six eligible husbands! Fanny is settled, of course, thank goodness, and my two youngest are still in the schoolroom; but there are these three to establish creditably."

Lady Nevern cast an approving glance at the Denham girls, who were gathered around the pianoforte. They certainly made an attractive picture. Louisa's white gown accentuated the fairness of her skin, and showed her slim figure to advantage. Catherine was bending over some music, so that the candles on the pianoforte caught the bright tints of her chestnut ringlets; and Eleanor's expressive face was full of vitality.

"There should be no difficulty," she said, consolingly. "They are all that they should be — charming in person and disposition alike. But then there's no reason why they should not be. You were a belle in your day, Sophia — I think perhaps Louisa has most the look of you, because she is of the same colouring, although the other two have something of your cast of countenance."

Lady Denham laughed deprecatingly. "Well, you were an acknowledged beauty yourself, my dear, so possibly you may be allowed to be a judge! Do you recall how Tadworth and Acton fought a duel over you, and —"

"Let us not revive old memories," interrupted Ariadne Nevern, hastily. "What is to be done now, Sophie? If James goes to Brighton, I have little hope that he will return here for more than a few days before going back to his house in Town."

Lady Denham hesitated. "As far as that goes," she said, slowly, "my girls have been promised to their sister in Brighton for some time — in fact, I must confess that I deferred their visit on receiving your note telling me that James was to come to you. They were a trifle disappointed at having to put Fanny off, so there should be no difficulty at all in persuading them to go to her, after all."

"Why, that is capital!" exclaimed Lady Nevern. "And perhaps, dearest Sophie, this little affair may go on better without our presence. Young people do not like to be pushed — but I am persuaded you don't need me to tell you that."

Chapter VI: The Donkey Ride

"Oh, no, oh, no! Pray do not — I don't wish to be dipped! I don't, I tell you! It's by far too rough! Put me down instantly!"

"There, me pretty dear," soothed Martha Gunn, the bathing woman, as she held the squirming figure in its long flannel smock over the foaming billows crashing on the beach. "You'll soon get used to it, an' it does ye a power o' good. There, now."

As she spoke, she lowered her writhing burden into the sea. The victim let out an anguished scream. At the sound of this, a head peeped nervously out from one of the blue bathing boxes which stood nearby.

"Oh, dear," said the owner of the head, in tremulous tones, "Is it so very bad, Celia?"

But the lady addressed was far too busy screaming to make any reply. Her open mouth took in a quantity of seawater, and she began to choke and cough. The face at the door of the bathing box paled visibly, and was quickly withdrawn.

Four ladies who had been strolling along the East Cliff and whose attention had been drawn by the screams, stood leaning against the railings which separated the road from the beach, watching. The eldest of them, an attractive young matron in a cherry coloured walking dress and a straw bonnet, laughed heartlessly.

"We must take you down there one morning," she said to her companions. "Wouldn't you like to try it, Katie?"

"Me?" replied her sister, heedless of grammar. "You must be in jest, Fanny! Why, sooner than find myself at the mercy of that dreadful old harpy in the blue jacket, I would — I don't know what, but something quite extreme, at all events!"

"That's Martha Gunn," explained Frances Hailsham. "She's the most experienced of all the bathing women, and quite a character. She dips the ladies, and old Smoaker Miles looks after the gentlemen. They bathe from the other side, of course. There's a tale about old Smoaker that he once pulled the Prince of Wales out by his ear because he thought His Royal Highness was venturing in too far. He said he'd no wish to be hanged for letting the heir to the throne drown, or at least that's the story as John told it to me."

"They look such frights, don't they?" asked Eleanor, as the four sisters continued to gaze at the unhappy female bathers. "Those dreary garments make them appear for all the world like corpses in their shrouds!"

"Ugh!" exclaimed Louisa, with a shiver.

"My dear Nell, have you ever heard of a screaming corpse?" asked Catherine, derisively.

"Oh, well, you know what I mean. But just look at that coal brig unloading its cargo right beside the bathing machines! I dare say those poor females will come out of the sea looking like blackamoors! Can they not do it somewhere else, Fanny?"

"Oh, they generally unload here; only Martha hasn't been able to take the machines right out into the sea today, as it's so rough. There's always something or other unloading on the beach. Sometimes it's fish," she added, wrinkling her nose. "And at other times, horses and carriages from the packet boats."

"Oh, do look!" exclaimed Eleanor, tugging at Fanny's arm suddenly. "See, there are some females riding on donkeys — how famous! Oh, where do you hire them, Fanny? I must — I positively must ride one! Aren't they sweet?"

Half a dozen or so donkeys with ladies sitting on their backs, were ambling along the beach in the direction of the bathing machines. They appeared to be in the care of a ragged urchin of nine or ten years old, who carried a whip.

"Yes, aren't they?" agreed Fanny, following her sister's gaze. "Well, if you'd care for a ride, Nell, there is no more to do than to step down on to the beach and tell the boy in charge of the animals."

"No, really?" demanded Eleanor, eagerly. "Oh, do let us go! Now — at once! You will come, won't you?"

She turned expectantly to the others, but they showed a disappointing lack of enthusiasm.

"Is it quite proper, Fanny, do you think?" asked Louisa.

"Lord, yes," replied her sister, easily. "Everyone does all manner of things at the seaside. Besides, all the fashionables will be strolling on the Steyne at this hour — you need not fear being observed by anyone of our acquaintance."

"You must excuse me," said Catherine. "Equestrian exercise is not my forte, as I know you'll agree, Nell. Besides, we're not dressed for riding."

"Oh, nonsense!" exclaimed Eleanor. "Donkeys are the most sedate of creatures — even you can't fall foul of one. As for dress, what in the world does that matter? These walking dresses will answer well enough."

"All of you go," urged Frances, "and I'll stay and watch you from here. It is only a short trot, you know, and won't occupy more than a few minutes."

Louisa and Catherine still demurred; but Eleanor, always eager to press any new scheme, finally managed by an adroit mixture of bullying and cajolery to persuade them. They left Frances and moved off, still disputing, in the direction of a slipway which led down to the beach.

A gentleman coming out of the Old Ship Hotel, which was situated almost opposite the point where the young ladies had been standing, paused a moment to watch the group. A flash of recognition came into his eyes; after a moment's hesitation he crossed the road and approached Frances, who stood looking after her sisters.

He removed his hat and bowed. "How do you do, Mrs. Hailsham? It is some time since we met, so possibly you won't remember me. I am Pamyngton."

She turned towards him, her eyes travelling over the tall, elegant figure in the well-fitting dark green coat and fawn pantaloons.

"Of course," she exclaimed, smiling and extending her hand. "I had a letter from Mama telling me that you were staying with your parents at Nevern Hall when she visited there recently. It *is* a long time since we met, is it not? It was at my wedding, I believe — oh, dear, how time does run on!"

"And how is your husband, ma'am? And your family — if my memory serves me, you have two children."

"Oh, they are all in excellent health, I thank you, sir! Are you in Brighton for the Races?"

He nodded. "I'm putting up at the Ship. I see your sisters are here with you, Mrs. Hailsham. I had the pleasure of meeting them for the first time when your parents dined with my family last week. They seem to have deserted you for the moment. Can I have the honour of escorting you somewhere?"

"I am only strolling along to the point where the donkey rides start," she replied with a smile. "My sisters have decided to try their skill."

He raised his brows. "What, even Miss Catherine? I understood that she was not addicted to riding, whether horses or donkeys."

"Well, I must admit she didn't seem over eager for the treat. But Nell had quite set her heart on it, and she would have called Katie a spoil-sport, which is not to be endured, of course."

"Indeed not," he assented gravely, falling into step beside her. "Do you suppose the young ladies would have any objection to my watching them at their sport, or would it be more tactful on my part to go away?"

"By no means," said Frances quickly, mindful of certain other matters which Mama had mentioned in her letter. "If you have nothing more pressing to do, Lord Pamyngton, I shall be very glad of your company, for it is tedious work laughing on one's own, besides appearing very odd to an onlooker."

"You think the spectacle may prove amusing?" he asked, smiling. "Oh dear, then perhaps I had better not stay. You may be permitted to laugh at your sisters, ma'am, but I can hardly expect to be accorded the same privilege. And already —" he made a rueful grimace — "I fear I have had the misfortune to displease Miss Catherine."

"Displease Katie?" Frances shot a keen look at him. "I cannot believe that — she is the most easy going girl in the world, and you must know you have considerable address, sir! Pray, what was your fault?"

"Well, possibly she may tell you about it herself, some time. But I think this is far enough along. See, they are about to mount now."

They both turned their attention to the group on the beach gathered round the donkeys.

The impetuous Eleanor had already perched herself on a donkey's back, and Louisa was being assisted into the saddle by the ragged urchin in charge of the pack. One or two other females were also mounting without any difficulty. Catherine and her donkey, however, stood eyeing each other with mutual distrust.

"Wretched creature!" said Catherine, softly, taking the reins in her hands and preparing to mount. "I know very well you are plotting all kinds of baleful things in that stupid head of yours!"

The donkey continued staring disdainfully at her, but made no protest when she finally managed to settle herself on its back. Slightly encouraged by this, she adjusted the folds of her yellow walking dress in a more seemly manner, and made sure her bonnet was not askew.

"Gee up!" shouted the urchin, flicking his whip through the air.

The donkeys, each with its precious burden, started forward at a sedate pace that could not possibly have alarmed the most nervous female. One animal, however, did not budge — the donkey on which Catherine was mounted.

"Oh, go on, you silly creature, go on!" she cried, drumming her heels against its sides, and jerking at the reins.

The donkey remained adamant. The other animals were now trotting placidly on the accustomed ride, steadily increasing the distance between themselves and the immobile member of their troop. Catherine redoubled her efforts, but it was all in vain. Her animal obstinately refused to move.

A laugh broke from Frances. Pamyngton glanced reproachfully at her, a smile trembling on his own lips.

"Oh, no, it's too bad of you, ma'am. Your poor sister must feel so put out. I wonder if that lad happens to have a carrot about him? That might do the trick."

At that moment, the donkey boy noticed his client's predicament, and turned back to assist her. He did not possess a carrot, but he did hold a whip. He used it generously.

Stung, the donkey emitted a bray and hurtled forward. Unprepared for this burst of activity, Catherine slipped, clawed desperately at the donkey's mane, and with a faint scream, fell to the ground. The donkey took no heed of its rider's fate, but went galloping onwards, never stopping until it had drawn level with the others.

Pamyngton let out an exclamation. The next moment he ducked under the railings, jumped down to the beach, and was running to Catherine's side. So were a number of other people, including the donkey boy, who was afraid of getting into trouble.

Pamyngton reached her first, just as she was struggling into an upright position.

"Are you hurt, Miss Catherine?" he asked, anxiously.

She turned her head and stared at him in amazement. She was a little shaken, but not at all hurt, having had the good fortune to land on a sandy patch instead of on the pebbles. By now, quite a little crowd was gathering; but she ignored everyone except Pamyngton, continuing to stare at him until recognition slowly showed in her eyes.

"So it's you, is it?" she said, resentfully, when she could recover her breath. "I might have known it! It only wanted that!"

Other voices now joined in, asking her how she was, and if she had broken any bones. She brushed the queries aside disdainfully, and started to rise.

"Allow me to assist you," said Pamyngton, quickly offering her his hands so that she might pull herself up.

"Thank you, no," she replied, in chilling tones. "I can manage perfectly well by myself."

This proved to be untrue. Her skirts had twisted round her when she fell, and were awkward to manage. She made several abortive attempts before at last he stepped forward, and placing an arm about her waist with a murmured apology, helped her to her feet.

She glared at him ungratefully. "Thank you," she said. "I dare say you might have arranged all this with that diabolical animal. You are kindred spirits, if ever I saw any!"

Pamyngton was wise enough to make no answer to this beyond a rueful smile. By now, Louisa and Eleanor had joined their sister, and were treating the incident each in her own characteristic way.

"Well, of all the ham-handed females I ever did see!" exclaimed Eleanor in disgust. "Can't even keep your seat on a poor little donkey — for shame, Kate!"

Louisa was anxious to make sure that her sister was not hurt. Frances, who had hurried down to the beach by the slipway and joined them at that moment, soon satisfied everyone on that point by a brief, but thorough, examination.

"Raise your arm, Katie, so — does that hurt? No? Now the other. Now walk forward a few steps. You feel no pain? You're sure? Anyway, we will get Dr. Bransome to look at you when we reach home, but I think you have taken no harm."

"No harm at all," said Catherine, impatiently. "Pray do not fuss, Fanny."

"It was that boy's fault," declared one of the bystanders. "He whipped the donkey hard, and the poor, dumb beast jumped with the pain, and so flung the young lady from his back."

"That beast may be dumb," remarked Catherine, grimly, "but his silences are eloquent. Evidently he's a creature of action rather than utterance."

"Please, ma'am," protested the donkey boy, who had paled slightly, "'twern't my fault, really it weren't. I allus gives 'em a touch of the whip when they're stubborn — Master says to do it — an' never before has one leapt off like that. An' now if ye're to tell Master what's 'appened, ma'am — y'r honour —" this was to Pamyngton — "it's me as'll get a leatherin', an' likely the sack to go with it."

His thin, young face looked appealingly into Pamyngton's.

"What do you say, Miss Catherine?" asked Pamyngton. "Do you want this young rascal brought to book?"

She glanced at the boy, and her expression softened. "No. No, I don't. It's nothing, really — I wish you wouldn't all fuss. Anyway, the boy can't be blamed. It's the fault of that stupid animal, and I suppose —" here she grinned ruefully — "myself, for not being a better rider."

"Very well, my lad, you can go. Have no fear, we shan't complain to your master. But next time you apply your whip, make sure it's not too hard." He held out his hand and slipped a coin into the boy's grubby palm. "That's all."

The donkey boy cut short his thanks on hearing the tone of dismissal. Like most lads who had been obliged to earn a living from an early age, he knew how far to push his good fortune. He swiftly shepherded the donkeys away; and the crowd, disappointed that events had not turned out more dramatically, dispersed almost as quickly as it had gathered.

"If you ladies would care to rest for a while, ma'am," said Pamyngton, addressing Frances, "you are very welcome to make use of my private parlour at the Ship."

"Why, thank you, sir," Frances was beginning, then broke off at the sight of Catherine's face. "I believe we must not trouble you," she went on, smoothly. "We are only five minutes' walk from home."

"Then perhaps I may escort you there?"

"You are very good, Lord Pamyngton, but it seems a pity to take you out of your way. But I hope that you will call on us sometime in West Street, and renew your acquaintance with my husband," she went on, in defiance of Catherine's dark looks. "It has been a pleasure to meet you again, and thank you once more for coming to my sister's aid."

He bowed. "I am happy to have been of service," he said, with what to Catherine seemed suspicious gravity. "And I shall certainly do myself the honour of calling on you."

He did not linger but took his leave gracefully. Frances looked after him for a moment, reflecting how well he carried himself and what an agreeable man he was. Then she turned to Catherine.

"You puzzle me, Katie. You seem as though you'd taken that charming man in dislike — come to think of it, he said he feared that he'd annoyed you, though he would not tell me how. Pray, how can he possibly have offended you?"

Catherine did not reply.

"You may well ask," put in Eleanor. "There is some secret between them, but neither of them will tell."

Catherine shrugged. "Oh, do stop talking nonsense, and let me go home!" she exclaimed. "My dress is ruined — it's all dirty and I've torn the hem! I feel a fright!"

"It's very fortunate that you aren't hurt," Louisa reminded her. "When I saw you about to fall, I had difficulty in suppressing a scream."

"Oh, pooh! No one can get hurt falling from a donkey!" scoffed Eleanor.

"Not I, certainly," agreed Catherine wryly. "I'm far too used to falling off horses' backs! No, the only thing that's hurt is my dignity, and I dare say that will mend."

Chapter VII: New Acquaintances

When they reached home, they found that both Masters of Ceremonies in the town, Mr. Wade of the Castle Inn and Mr. Yart of the Old Ship, had called and left their cards.

"Oh," remarked Fanny, picking these up and setting them down again, "they only wish to place your names in their book, so that they can make arrangements for you to attend the assemblies. However, I believe we can dispense with their good offices, for John will introduce you to enough officers to provide you with three or four partners apiece, I promise you. Indeed, if you're looking for husbands, my dears, you could be very well suited in Brighton! That reminds me — talking of husbands, which of you is to have Pamyngton? I understand from Mama that Lady Nevern is quite determined it should be one of you."

"Nell," replied Catherine, promptly. "She's in love with his house — oh, and his title."

"Well, at least there's no mystery about *my* dealings with the gentleman," retorted Eleanor, darkly.

"How intriguing all this talk of a mystery is!" exclaimed Frances, with relish. "Come, Kate, you can't be so unkind as not to enlighten us."

"Oh, you know Nell," replied Catherine, airily. "She loves to dramatize things."

"Do I?" demanded Eleanor. "Well, how do you account for the fact that he recognized you that day when we met him on our way to the village, and yet we had none of us ever set eyes on him before? Or at least," she amended, in a teasing tone, "we were none of us *supposed* ever to have met him before.

Louisa and I had not, at all events. Yes, and when we dined with the Neverns you were behaving most oddly towards him — you noticed it, too, didn't you, Lou?"

"Well," admitted Louisa, reluctantly. "I must confess there did seem to be something in your manner, Katie, towards Lord Pamyngton that evening. You had not quite your usual self-assurance."

"Oh, Katie, this is all too tantalizing! Pray do let us into the secret," begged Frances, eagerly. "Had you met him before? When? Where? How? Tell us all!"

"Nell can tell you a deal better than I can, because it all exists in her imagination," said Catherine with a shrug. "I'm going upstairs to change my gown."

"I wonder what she is concealing?" asked Eleanor, after her sister had left the room.

"Well, if she doesn't wish to tell us," remarked Louisa, "it's not very kind to pry. One likes to keep some matters to oneself, after all."

"Do you suppose she can be in love with him?" mused Frances, whose curiosity was as lively as Eleanor's.

"Goodness, no!" replied Eleanor. "Nothing of that kind! It's more as if she's harbouring some kind of grudge against him. I know she was furious when Mama said we might not come and stay with you while Lord Pamyngton remained at Nevern Hall, and I wondered at first if it might be that. But you know how quickly Katie recovers from a pet; and anyway it all turned out right in the end, for luckily Mr. Eversley persuaded Lord Pamyngton to come to Brighton himself. I've puzzled my wits, but I can't think of anything else; but I know that those two have certainly met before, and you may depend that something must have happened between them. But what?" she finished, throwing up her hands in exasperation. "And why won't she tell us? She's always told us everything before!"

"Well, don't let it vex you," said Frances, soothingly. "No doubt she'll confide in you when she's ready."

But Catherine was certainly not ready to confide in anyone yet about her dealings with Viscount Pamyngton. If she could have laughed over them, it would have been a different matter; but she still felt foolish and just a little angry. It had been unpardonable of him to deceive her in that way, leading her on to say things which even now could make her blush, whenever she recalled them. The donkey incident had not helped, either. It seemed she was destined to cut a foolish figure in his eyes. Nothing could more successfully set a girl against a man.

In the afternoon, Colonel Hailsham and Frances took the three girls for a stroll on the crowded Steyne, Brighton's fashionable parade. It was a gay scene; the pastel shades of the ladies' muslins contrasted pleasantly with the more sober hues of the gentlemen's coats, which were mostly of dark blue or forest green, with here and there a dash of military red. A band was playing 'Nancy Dawson', and the sun shone down with warm approval over all.

"That's old Phoebe Hassell," remarked John Hailsham, as they passed a fruit and gingerbread stall tended by a comical looking old woman dressed in a rusty black cloak and a bonnet with a red and white spotted neckerchief tied under it. "She's a well-known character in Brighton — a rum story, hers."

At once, the three girls clamoured for details.

"I'll tell you," said Frances. "She fell in love with a soldier — a common enough fate in this town —" here she gave her husband a saucy look not often seen on the face of a woman who had been a wife for five years — "and when his regiment was ordered abroad, she actually disguised herself as a man and enrolled in the Army herself, so that she could follow him."

Her sisters exclaimed incredulously at this.

"But how in the world could she possibly manage to deceive everyone in that way?" asked Catherine. "I should have thought —"

Louisa nudged her, fearful of what she might say next in front of their brother-in-law. Catherine stifled a gurgle of laughter, and obediently subsided.

"As to that, I can't say," went on Frances. "But she fought alongside the other soldiers, and was actually wounded at the battle of Fontenoy. Her lover was wounded, too, though more severely, so that he had to be sent home; but she confided her story to the General's lady, and was given a discharge so that she could follow him. Once they were at home, she nursed him back to health, and later on they were married. There! Don't you find it a romantic story?"

"She doesn't look particularly romantic," said Eleanor, doubtfully, with a sidelong glance at the old woman. "Is it really true, or are you roasting us, Fanny?"

"Perfectly true, I assure you," replied the Colonel.

"Well, perhaps you may not look so very romantic at that age," said Fanny. "But look, there is Sir John Lade, driving that tilbury. He's in charge of the Royal Stables, and a great favourite with the Prince."

"What, that odd little man!" exclaimed Catherine. "He's like an undersized groom, not a bit distinguished looking at all!"

"Be careful," warned Fanny, lowering her voice. "It does not do to criticize the Prince's entourage. Besides, he's not at all objectionable. Now his wife is another matter. Before she married Sir John, she was under the protection of the Duke of

York, and she's as foul-mouthed a female as I ever want to meet. Yet she's always included in the Pavilion parties."

"Letitia Lade?" queried John Hailsham, making a wry face. "One thing I will say in her favour, she's a first-rate whip — said to be the foremost lady horsewoman in the country, y'know."

"Evidently a rival to our Katie!" remarked Eleanor with a laugh.

They had now reached Donaldson's library, but decided to resist its many attractions for the moment, as the young ladies were eager to have their first view of the Pavilion. Two gentlemen in military coats who were just coming out of the library saluted Colonel Hailsham. He stopped and introduced them to his family as Captain North and Captain Crendon.

Captain North was a stringy looking young man with a slightly vacuous expression and an irritatingly high-pitched laugh. The other officer, who was a year or two older, was dark, with heavy eyebrows which suggested an autocratic will, and a slightly sardonic smile. He seemed to be a man of few words; but Captain North had a light, easy flow of conversation which quickly recommended him to Eleanor.

Seeing this, John Hailsham invited the two officers to join the party, and they all strolled on towards the Pavilion, finding it difficult to keep together because of the press of people. Presently they left the paved walk inside the railings of the Steyne to stand in the carriage road so that they could obtain a better view.

The Pavilion had originally been built on the conventional Palladian plan of a central Rotunda with two flanking wings. Some alterations had recently been made; there were now two additional wings placed at right angles to the existing building, and green canopies had been erected over all the windows.

"Well," said the Colonel to Louisa, "what do you think of it, eh?"

"Oh, I like it! It is exactly my idea of a summer palace. The bow windows, and those little wrought iron balconies, give it such an elegant appearance! It is so very fitting for an English coastal town, I think."

"More like Cathay inside, ma'am," remarked Captain North, with one of his high-pitched laughs. "Chinese wallpaper, Chinese furniture, Chinese lanterns — regular touch of the Orient, what, Crendon?"

"The passage along the southern wing is certainly as you describe it," replied Captain Crendon.

"No, really?" said Catherine, eagerly.

"Assure you, ma'am," answered Captain North. "I understand it all started with some Chinese wallpaper that someone or other gave Prinney. Dashed odd, too, for chinoiserie's been out of date for years, what? But dashed if he don't think now that it would be a good notion to do the whole place up in Oriental style, outside and in! All I can say is, I'd like to see it, what?"

"Oh, and so would I!" exclaimed Eleanor. "What a capital notion!"

"Capital," remarked Captain Crendon, dryly, "is precisely what's lacking to carry out such a scheme. His Royal Highness is never beforehand with the world, I fear."

"All the same," said Catherine, "I do hope we have an opportunity of viewing the interior."

"Of course you will," Frances assured her. "We are sure to be asked to one of the musical parties before long. John and I have been there several times, though not so frequently of late, for Mrs. Fitzherbert has been trying to persuade the Prince to live a little more quietly since his illness last year. But there are always banquets and parties in Race Week, and next month there'll be the Prince's birthday celebrations, too."

Eleanor sighed with contentment. "Oh, how glad I am that we were able to come to Brighton!" she exclaimed.

"So are we, ma'am," retorted Captain North, gallantly. "Deuced glad, what? Eh, Crendon?"

"Oh, undoubtedly," replied the other.

Catherine smiled at his dry tone and gave him one of her saucy looks. He raised his dark brows a trifle.

"Most decidedly," he amended, studying her thoughtfully until she turned away, a little confused.

"Well, I hope you have looked at the Pavilion your fill," said the Colonel, moving over towards the two younger girls. "Shall we move on?"

They assented, and the party strolled back down the Steyne, past the Castle Inn, which was pointed out to them by Frances.

"That's where the Grand Race Ball is to be held next week," she said. "It's the first Assembly of the season and will be opened by the Prince, so you may depend it will be a grand occasion. But I dare say your season in London last year will have quite spoilt you for balls."

"How can you say so?" demanded Eleanor, indignantly. "For my part, I can never have too much of dancing."

"Egad, you are right, ma'am," declared Captain North, with a laugh. "What better occupation can there be for the fair sex than to delight us poor menfolk with such grace, such elegance as may be readily displayed in a ballroom? Where else are we privileged to behold beauty at her most entrancing, what? Don't you agree, Crendon, eh?"

This time, Captain Crendon said nothing; but his eyes met Catherine's, and they both started to laugh.

"Ay, you may laugh at me, you good-for-nothing fellow," chided his friend, "but I'll wager you're of my opinion for all that, what?"

"You make it difficult for Captain Crendon to disagree with you, sir," remarked Catherine, saucily. "If he does so, he must seem ungallant."

"Why, so he is," replied Captain North. "A regular boor of a chap, assure you, ma'am. I quite despair of him at times, I can tell you. But I'm determined to persevere, and try if I can't make something of him yet."

Captain Crendon gave an ironical bow. "Now you have my character, ladies. Some time I must give you my opinion of North's — but I shall wait until he is not by."

"Oh, but he is in jest, you know," said Eleanor, who in spite of her quick perception could sometimes be a little naïve.

This made Catherine and Captain Crendon laugh again. The Colonel, who had not heard much of the preceding conversation, as he had been busy talking to his wife and Louisa, threw them a sharp look.

He moved across to Captain Crendon's side, and Catherine found herself edged out to walk beside Frances and Louisa for a little way.

"What do you think of the two officers?" asked Frances, in a low tone.

"Oh, they are very agreeable," replied Catherine, "but I wish Captain North would not laugh so much. He has such a stupid laugh."

"You seemed not to find Captain Crendon's laugh at all disagreeable," remarked Frances, slyly.

"I should judge him to be a more sensible man," put in Louisa.

"Sensible? Well, it depends. He has rather the reputation of being a neck-or-nothing fellow, as John says, and a bit of a womanizer into the bargain. Not that we know any real harm of him," she added, fair-mindedly. "Oh, but look over there! Here comes someone whom we all know."

"Who? Where?" asked Catherine, looking about her.

"Over there, just beyond those two elderly ladies sharing one parasol, one of them wearing a frightful purple gown! A group against the railings — four gentlemen — two of them in riding dress — no, do not stare so, Katie!"

Catherine, having identified Viscount Pamyngton among the group, was only too anxious to obey this behest. At this moment, Eleanor eluded Captain North and moved to her sister's side, leaving the three officers talking together.

"Have you noticed?" she demanded of them. "There is Mr. Eversley over there, with Lord Pamyngton! How very fortunate if they speak to us, for I would like to renew my acquaintance with Mr. Eversley. He is a prodigiously entertaining young man!"

"Be quiet, Nell!" admonished Catherine, in a whisper. "If you stare so, they are sure to notice us and stop to speak."

"And why in the world shouldn't they?" asked Eleanor, in astonishment. "It is the very thing I would like — besides, Mama didn't send us here to *avoid* Lord Pamyngton, as you very well know."

"Well, really, you are the stupidest girl —!" began Catherine, in an irritated voice.

She was not allowed to say more, for as their group drew level with Pamyngton's, he removed his hat and stepped forward to address Frances. Frederick Eversley, too, bowed in the direction of the three Denham girls, and general introductions followed.

In such a large group, it was not possible for long to avoid splitting up into twos and threes; and soon Catherine found herself talking to Captain Crendon again. After a while Pamyngton appeared at her elbow, but she took care to appear completely absorbed in her conversation with the Captain.

Pamyngton continued to wait patiently by her, addressing an odd remark to one or another of the party as the occasion demanded. Then, when Captain Crendon's attention was claimed for a moment by the Colonel, he seized the opportunity to say, in a low tone, "I trust you are none the worse for your little accident of this morning, Miss Catherine."

She reddened a trifle. "Oh, not at all!" she said, airily. "I have forgotten it completely."

"I could wish your memory were as short for the offences of humans as it evidently is for those of animals," he said, with a quizzical smile.

"But animals, my lord," she retorted, quickly, "offend without knowing what they do."

"You may be right, Miss Catherine, yet I had the oddest notion this morning that your donkey was very well aware of what he was doing."

She shrugged, but made no answer.

"Is there no penance I can do to expiate my fault?" he asked, in mock humility. "You cannot mean to punish me in this way for ever."

"I have nothing to add to what I said before, my lord."

He sighed. "Oh, dear! Since you keep calling me 'my lord', I see there is very little hope. I wonder what I can possibly do to mend matters?"

He gazed at her thoughtfully for a moment with such a plaintive expression that she was hard put to it not to laugh.

"I have it!" he exclaimed suddenly, on a triumphant note. "Now, why did I not think of that before?"

She opened her lips as though she would speak, then shut them again firmly, determined not to be betrayed into showing the slightest curiosity.

He smiled, and was beginning to say something else, when he was interrupted by Captain Crendon, who had turned to address her again.

Reluctantly, she transferred her attention to the Captain. She was quite surprised to find that in some curious way she had been enjoying this interchange with Pamyngton.

Chapter VIII: Flowers in Season

"The most intriguing thing, Katie!" exclaimed Frances, bursting into the morning room where the three girls were sitting shortly after breakfast on the following day. "Something has arrived for you — a —" she stopped, and laughed. "But I'll not say any more," she resumed. "It shall be a surprise! Come and see!"

With one accord, her sisters jumped to their feet and almost pushed her through the open door.

"What is it? Do tell us — don't be tiresome, Fanny! Did you say for Katie? What can it be?"

Their eager questions made her laugh again as she guided them to a table in the hall. On it stood a large wicker basket containing a profusion of roses in every hue, their perfume filling the air. The sisters gasped and stared.

"For me?" asked Catherine, at last. "How do you know?"

Frances indicated a small envelope fastened to the handle of the basket. Catherine advanced to take it in her hand and saw that her name was inscribed on it.

She pulled it away from the fastening, and tore it open with mounting curiosity. It contained a very small card with a brief message: 'Alas, they are not out of season. I fear it is one more fault for which I must beg your forgiveness.'

There was no signature. She stared as the colour mounted to her cheeks.

"Well, who is it?" demanded Eleanor, impatiently. "Aren't you going to tell us who sent them?"

Catherine shook her head. "The card isn't signed," she said, still regarding it thoughtfully.

"Not signed?" echoed Eleanor. "But there's something written on it, isn't there? I can see that from here!"

"Even if it isn't signed," remarked Frances, studying her sister's face, "I think you know very well who sent the flowers."

"Perhaps," replied Catherine, slowly.

"Well, there's no need to make a mystery of it, is there?" demanded her younger sister, indignantly. "Surely you can tell us? Is it Captain Crendon? The two of you were going along famously yesterday, I must say. I'll wager it's he!"

But Catherine ungenerously declined to satisfy their curiosity. She picked up the basket, and saying that she would take it to her room, abruptly left them standing there in the hall. As she mounted the staircase, she could hear them discussing her attitude in far from flattering terms.

When she reached her bedroom, she placed the basket on the dressing table, and sat down pensively before it. The card was still in her hand. She read it again.

It was from Pamyngton, there could be no doubt of that. But what did he mean by it? 'Alas, they are not out of season.' She had realized at once that this was a reference to one of her own foolish, impetuous remarks at that first meeting, when she had stated emphatically that the man she married must prove his love by sending her flowers that were out of season. Was he flirting with her, or could he possibly be attempting to pay her serious attentions? She shook her head at this thought, and a saucy smile curved her mouth. She could no more believe in the earnestness of his attentions than she could in his much-vaunted penitence for deceiving her about his name. It seemed the gentleman had a talent for nonsense, and nonsense of this kind was very much to Catherine's taste. She recalled the entertainment she had found in yesterday's brief conversation with him, and how sorry she had been when it ended. Yes, and now she came to think of it, he had said something then which might account for this gift of flowers today. Well, if that was the game he chose to play, she was not unwilling. It might be amusing to pursue it for a time. The question was, should she share the jest with her sisters?

She pondered this point for a while. It might be awkward to keep it from them; if Pamyngton continued his light-hearted pursuit of her, they might take it for earnest, and report it to Mama. She shuddered at the thought of the complications and embarrassments which might arise from this. Besides, a joke shared was usually a joke doubled. What finally decided her was the sudden discovery that she no longer resented the deception he had practised on her. At first, the recollection of it had made her feel foolish, but now all such embarrassment had passed away. She was ready to admit, if only to herself, that he had perhaps had a certain amount of justification for concealing his identity. However that might be, the episode had lost its sting. She was ready to laugh over it, and to derive added entertainment from keeping up a pretence of still being vexed with him.

So when her three sisters eventually followed her upstairs, they found her in a carefree mood and quite ready to share her story with them. Louisa at first showed a tendency to be shocked by this recital of her sister's indiscretions; but the other two so evidently found it amusing that she soon joined in their merriment, even if in a more restrained way.

"I knew you'd been up to something that day, Katie," declared Eleanor, laughing, "but I never guessed the half! Running away — and on Stella! You might have known she wouldn't let you ride her far, you goose! And to be rescued by Viscount Pamyngton, of all people!"

"You know," said Frances, reflectively, "Mama herself could not have arranged anything better suited to her purpose. Only consider the outcome. He is evidently taken with you."

"Nonsense!" exclaimed Catherine, colouring a little. "It's just a game — he's not serious."

"How can you be sure?" demanded Louisa.

Catherine shrugged. "Oh I don't know, but I am. His manner is altogether too light-hearted — perhaps he's flirting a little, but no more. And I don't mind confessing that I mean to join him in the game, too — it will be vastly diverting! For a time, at any rate, that is."

"Oh, Katie!" said Louisa, reproachfully.

"Well, why not? You must know, Lou, that I'm not nearly so serious-minded as you are. And I think it would be no bad thing if you were to stop brooding over Oliver for a while, and indulge in a little harmless flirtation with someone or other. There are plenty of handsome young officers in Brighton. What do you say to Captain Crendon, for instance?"

"I've no desire to flirt with that gentleman or anyone else," replied Louisa, firmly.

"Well, I must say I agree with Katie," put in Eleanor. "Where is the use in mooning away after a man you may never wed? You don't wish to be an old maid, do you, now?"

"My wishes have nothing to say to the matter," muttered Louisa, with a trembling lip.

"Well, I'll not believe that even Oliver could wish such a fate on you," retorted Eleanor, with more persistence than tact. "He has positively no prospect of advancement, and nothing less would reconcile Papa and Mama to your marriage, so surely he must see that the only course is for you both to look about you for someone else."

"Well, really!" began Frances. "Of all the cold-blooded little monsters —!"

"She doesn't understand," said Louisa, quietly. "How could she? But allow me to tell you, Nell, that Oliver has done exactly what you think he should. At our last meeting —" her lips quivered for a moment — "he told me that I must try to forget him, and he said — he said — that he would do his best to overcome his feelings for me."

Catherine stared in amazement. "Well!" she exclaimed. "Whatever you may think of that, Lou, *I* call it uncommonly poor-spirited!"

Louisa bridled. "I will not have you say so! You have known Oliver all your life, as we all have. You cannot in justice accuse him of lacking any manly — or gentlemanly — quality!"

"Besides," put in Frances, reasonably, "what would you have him do?"

"Oh, something outrageous and — and impossible, and — romantic!" exclaimed Catherine. "I don't know what — defy Mama and Papa, and run off with you to Gretna Green!"

She burst out laughing at the effect of this utterance on her audience. Louisa was too stunned for speech, and even Eleanor looked taken aback. Frances, after a momentary look of disapproval, relaxed into an indulgent smile.

"Leaving on one side all questions of propriety, can you suppose such conduct would serve to advance him in his chosen profession? No, Katie, you'll have to do better than that."

"Of course I'm not serious. But all the same, I do think he takes the matter tamely — oh, very well, Lou! I'm sorry." She flung an arm about her sister, and kissed her cheek. "I'll not tease you any more, I promise. But since you have his permission to try and forget him, why not indulge in a little harmless flirtation? It has a prodigiously tonic effect, I assure you."

"You are a shameless minx!" said Frances, severely. "I can see that I shall have my hands full in chaperoning you."

Chapter IX: The Grand Rose Ball

The first Assembly of the season had been opened at half past nine by the Prince of Wales, his tightly corseted stomach threatening to burst the buttons of his elegant dark blue coat, and his fleshy face beaming with joviality. He had good reason to be pleased, for his horse, Orville, had come in first at the Races that day. The Prince had previously made a gift of a silver gilt cup which was to be presented to this years' winner; but as his own horse had won, he magnanimously presented the trophy to Orville's former owner.

The ballroom at the Castle Inn was a handsome one, lit by three magnificent glass chandeliers and decorated with pilasters which formed a series of compartments at each end of the room and along the sides. Here those who were not dancing might sit in comparative seclusion and watch the more active members of the assembly; or if they tired of this, could admire the classical paintings which adorned the walls.

Louisa and Catherine were sitting together on a sofa in one of these alcoves during an interval between the dances. They were so absorbed in watching Eleanor, who was standing some distance away conducting a lively conversation with a group of young people, that both of them gave a start when a gentleman approached unobserved to speak to them.

They looked round and saw it was Viscount Pamyngton. Catherine thought immediately how well he looked in his formal evening attire. His fair hair and complexion were admirably set off by the black coat and breeches which he was wearing with a waistcoat of quilted white marcella. He bowed and asked Louisa if she would do him the honour of dancing with him.

She seemed taken by surprise, and she declined hastily, in a confused way that might have been expected from a girl at her first ball, but was scarcely fitting in one of her years and social experience.

Pamyngton accepted her refusal with a good grace, and turned to solicit Catherine's hand instead. This had been his real object, but he was not the man to flout the proper forms; an elder sister must always be asked before a younger.

"Thank you, sir, but I am already engaged for the next dance," replied Catherine, glancing at him demurely from under her lashes.

"A pity. Then perhaps I may venture to hope for the following one?"

"Well, as to that, I'm sure I can't recall — but I am certain that I owe it to someone," she said, outrageously.

"If he is so unimportant that you've forgotten his name, Miss Catherine, then could you not go a little further and forget the engagement altogether?"

"Oh, no! That would be most improper," she said, in her most virtuous manner.

He bowed. "Of course I must not urge you to forsake the proprieties, ma'am. But perhaps if I apply to you again in the course of the evening, I may be fortunate enough to find you at liberty for just one dance?"

She unfurled her fan, and hid a smile behind it. "Perhaps — I cannot be sure. Oh, here comes my partner — you must forgive me."

She rose from the sofa as Captain Crendon came towards them. After a brief exchange of civilities, he escorted her to the floor.

Pamyngton allowed a small sigh to escape him. "Alas, I am deprived of both my partners," he said to Louisa with a rueful smile. "Can I not persuade you to change your mind, and take pity on me? Or are you, too, awaiting another and more welcome partner?"

"Oh, no," disclaimed Louisa, hastily. "I — I had no intention of dancing at all, my lord."

He raised his eyebrows. "No intention of dancing, ma'am? But surely that is a little singular. Why else does one attend a ball?"

Louisa coloured. "I came because — oh, because it was expected of me," she answered, hurriedly. "I had no expectation of pleasure from the occasion."

He considered her thoughtfully. "I must confess, Miss Denham, that I have never yet encountered a young lady who did not expect any pleasure from a ball. But perhaps my experience is not so wide as I had supposed. Or is it that I have so far been sadly deceived in thinking that these fair creatures we see before us —" he negligently waved his quizzing glass in the direction of the dancers — "are really enjoying themselves? Your sister, for instance, over there —" his roving glance found the laughing Catherine and her dark, handsome partner — "can it possibly be that her animated manner conceals a deep detestation of the whole business? You, who know her so well, must provide the answer. I can only say that she has tricked me completely into believing that she is enjoying herself prodigiously."

This speech won a reluctant laugh from Louisa. "Oh, yes, Katie is certainly enjoying herself! She always does, you know — she has excellent spirits. But then, there is no reason why she should not." She sighed. "She is heart whole and fancy free, very different —"

She pulled herself up abruptly, on the verge of an indiscreet admission.

"You would have said," prompted Pamyngton, gently, "from yourself. Am I right?"

She nodded miserably. He waited a moment, his eyes fixed on her in a look of understanding and compassion that almost tempted her to pour out all her troubles to him. She suddenly understood why it was that Katie had so recklessly confided in this man when he had found her stranded on the road to Cuckfield. When they had been told the story yesterday, all the sisters had protested at her indiscretion.

"I couldn't help it," Catherine had insisted. "There's something about him that draws you on to tell him everything — yet he's no Paul Pry, don't think that. It's just that he's so — oh, so prodigiously understanding! The French have a better word for it — *sympathique*."

Sympathique: yes, that was it exactly, thought Louisa. But her sense of propriety, always stronger than Catherine's, prevented her from following her sister's example in giving confidences which would later, no doubt, be regretted. She forced a smile.

"I dare say I am past the age for taking pleasure in balls," she said, with an attempt at lightness.

"Oh, undoubtedly," he agreed, cheerfully. "A lady of your advanced years clearly cannot be expected to dance, and should never venture out unless in a wheelchair. Have you tried a sojourn at Bath, ma'am? They say the waters there are most beneficial for the elderly. Brighton, I fear, is altogether too lively and bracing a place when one has reached the evening of life, as it were."

In spite of herself, Louisa could not help laughing. Having started, she found it not too difficult to continue, especially as her companion kept up a flow of witty nonsense which gave her no time for melancholy thoughts.

Catherine, passing close to them in the movements of the dance, noticed with amazement how well they seemed to be going on together. Louisa was actually laughing! That was indeed a rare happening nowadays. She kept her eyes on them for a while longer, and presently was astonished to see Pamyngton leading her sister on to the floor. An exclamation escaped her which made her partner turn his head in the direction of her incredulous gaze.

"What is it?" His bored glance lighted on Pamyngton, and a sneer came into his voice. "Never say that the amiable Pamyngton has roused your interest, Miss Catherine? If so, you can look to have a good many rivals, for I collect that he's quite the most eligible catch of the season."

"Certainly not!" exclaimed Catherine, with hauteur. "I wonder you should have the temerity to say such a thing to me!"

"I've plenty of temerity, one way and another, ma'am," he said with a sardonic smile, taking her hand to guide her through one of the movements of the dance. "And I rather think that you have, too. Perhaps that's why we make such splendid partners?"

"Perhaps." She flashed a quick smile at him, her good humour restored. "But, tell me, why do you dislike Lord Pamyngton?"

"Dislike?" He shook his head. "Too strong. The fellow's a bore — he's got altogether too much of everything. Too much affability, money, position — even too much luck."

"Too much luck?"

"Exactly. He cleaned up a packet at Raggett's t'other evening, and another at the Races today. Now I," he finished, with a dry smile, "can do nothing right in that direction lately. Lady Luck has deserted me for the moment. Like any woman, she's a fickle jade, and always bestows her favours where they're least appreciated."

"Raggett's?" queried Catherine. "I don't know — is that a gaming place?"

He nodded. "The play's devilish high there, too."

"Well, sir, I'm sorry if your luck is out for the moment. But perhaps Viscount Pamyngton has earned his — you know what the saying is —" she gave him a coy glance — "Lucky at cards, unlucky in love."

"Indeed?" The dark brows lifted. "I was not aware of any particular interest of his at present. But you ladies, of course, are always better informed on such matters."

"You are not very gallant to say so, Captain Crendon!"

"No," he replied, mockingly. "Do you mind?"

She tossed her head, and the chandelier above caught the chestnut lights in her hair.

"I wasn't speaking of now," she said, "but of the past — long past. I've been told that Lord Pamyngton was once very much in love with a girl who married someone else."

He frowned in an effort of concentration. "Ah, yes, I do recall something of the kind. I was only a young sprig then, though. It was one of the Eversley girls, was it not? A deuced fine redhead, like all of them — took London by storm, and ended up marrying some ineligible fellow or other. Is that the story?"

"Yes, that's it. So you see, sir, you must not grudge Lord Pamyngton his luck with cards and horses."

"I grudge the man nothing but his share in our conversation, which is far beyond his desserts. I would much prefer to talk about you. Has anyone ever told you how pretty your hair is?"

"I suppose the proper answer to that would be no," she said, with a saucy look. "But I am going to follow your lead in candour, Captain Crendon. Yes, I have been told so — several times."

He grinned. "You see, it's just as I said. We make capital partners. Will you drive out with me to Rottingdean tomorrow?"

"If my sister Fanny permits it." She was at her most demure now.

"She will. I shall seek her out as soon as this dance is over. And then I shall come to claim you for the next."

"You are very sure of yourself, sir, but it will not do. We cannot be dancing too much together, or people will talk."

"Pah! Gossip! You don't regard the old tabbies any more than I do."

She laughed, tapping him playfully on the wrist with her fan. Pamyngton and Louisa, who were close at hand at that moment, saw the gesture.

"Your sister appears tolerably pleased with her partner," remarked Pamyngton, thoughtfully.

Louisa agreed, watching the other couple for a moment.

"I wish I had his address," went on Pamyngton, with a rueful smile. "Whenever I approach Miss Catherine, we seem to be at odds in a second. You saw how she refused to dance with me."

"Oh, you must not heed Katie — it's just one of her little games," replied Louisa, consolingly. "She's full of fun, you know, and scarcely ever takes anything seriously."

"So I should suppose; but it does happen that unfortunately I have given her some cause to be vexed with me. Therefore I find it difficult to judge how much of her manner towards me is jest and how much earnest." He paused, then added, "I would rather like to know."

Her lovely blue eyes held a soft expression as they lifted to his face. "I don't think she is vexed with you any longer, my lord, though she may have been at first."

"You know about my offence, then? She has told you?"

Louisa nodded. "She told us yesterday. We had guessed there was something, but knew we should have to wait to find out about it until it no longer upset her. And that with Katie," she added, reflectively, "is never very long. So you see there's no occasion for you to concern yourself — you may forget the whole incident, as she has done."

"Oddly enough," he replied, quietly, "I don't wish to forget it. I found it most diverting. Your sister is an — unusual — young lady."

Louisa looked uneasy. "Yes — even her family seldom know what she would be at. I — forgive me, but I think you should not take her too seriously, sir — in any way." She invested the final words with significance. "She is very young and gay; and although she is the sweetest, most loving girl in the world, she can be a thought — heedless, at times."

"I take your meaning, Miss Denham." He gave her a serious look. "And I thank you for your interest."

"As to that," stammered Louisa, her colour coming and going, "I know what it is to be unhappy — that is to say, I would not have anyone — if anything I could say would prevent it —"

He pressed her hand. "I, too, am not without previous experience of that kind. Believe me, I am truly grateful for your warning."

But the question was, thought Louisa, did it come in time?

Chapter X: A Chance Meeting

Frances demurred a little at the proposed drive with Captain Crendon, but in the end she consented.

"It is not that there's anything singular in a gentleman driving a young lady to Rottingdean, for you may see any amount of curricles and phaetons on any fine day on that particular road. It is as respectable as a drive in Hyde Park. But I had far rather see you go with Pamyngton than with Captain Crendon, I must confess."

"But Lord Pamyngton hasn't asked me."

"Whose fault is that? I noticed that you refused to dance with him last night on several occasions. It was scarcely civil of you."

"Oh, well," said Catherine, with a shrug, "I was already promised to someone else for those particular dances, and it would have been even more uncivil to break a previous engagement, now, wouldn't it? Besides, he consoled himself with Lou!" She turned to Louisa. "I must say I was amazed to see you standing up with him — or, indeed, with anyone! But I was monstrous glad that you heeded my advice, after all."

A faint colour came to Louisa's cheek. "I did not like to refuse his second application, especially after you'd also refused him," she said, apologetically. "It must be vastly uncomfortable for a gentleman to be rebuffed in that way, and especially such a one as Viscount Pamyngton."

"Because he is a wealthy nobleman, you mean?" scoffed Catherine. "All the more reason why he should be made to understand that not every girl will come running at a crook of his little finger!"

"I do *not* mean that, for I'm positive that he is not the kind of gentleman to suppose anything of the kind," objected Louisa, with some heat. "What I meant was that — well, that —"

She hesitated.

"Well?" prompted Catherine.

"It is not his rank or fortune," continued Louisa, slowly, "but his other qualities, of which I am sure he's scarcely aware. He's such a fine-looking gentleman — it's not too much to call him handsome — and his air, manners and address are so exactly what they ought to be —"

"So they are," agreed Frances, watching her sister closely.

"He's had an expensive education," remarked Catherine, her tongue in her cheek.

"So have others, but with less desirable results," retorted Louisa. "The qualities one must particularly admire in Lord Pamyngton spring from his own character, and not from any artificially inspired cause. He is so understanding of the difficulties and shortcomings of others, so — so gentle, somehow —"

She broke off in confusion, realizing that her sisters were staring at her.

"In short, he's a paragon," summed up Catherine after a pause, dismissing the subject with a shrug. "And I never did care for paragons, not being one myself. Well, I must go and make ready for my outing."

Frances, too, declared that she must attend to some domestic business; both sisters wore thoughtful looks as they turned away.

Catherine's soon vanished as she conducted a lightning survey of her wardrobe for something to wear. Garments were flung hither and thither until her maid, who had been with her for some years and was allowed a great deal of freedom, uttered a protest.

"Sakes, Miss Katie, there'll not be one of those gowns fit to wear afterwards! Have done, do!"

But at that moment Catherine seized a pink and white striped muslin walking dress with a square neck and short, puff sleeves.

"My pink gloves and slippers, Betsy, quick, quick! Oh, I'm sorry it's all such a mess, but I'm in a prodigious rush! Pray, which bonnet shall I wear? This!" She held up a Grecian helmet, and surveyed it critically before flinging it down in a way which would have wounded her milliner to the quick — "No, I am not in the mood for classical simplicity today! It shall be this one, I think. It frames my face quite delightfully, besides having ribbons to match my gown! But my hair is such a mess — pray be a good girl, Betsy, and do my hair for me very quickly, please, and in your prettiest style! And I tell you what, I will give you my yellow gown that you admire so much, to wear when you go walking with that good-looking footman next door."

"A footman next door, miss?" asked Betsy, innocently. "Which one is that?"

"Don't think I haven't noticed you out with him, you sly thing," replied her mistress, hurriedly washing her hands and face in a bowl of warm, perfumed water.

Betsy was heard to say that a girl must take her diversions where she could find them, especially when she was away from her usual haunts.

"Very true," replied Catherine, drying herself on the towel which the maid handed to her. "That is precisely what I am myself doing."

Captain Crendon was chatting to Frances in the morning room when Catherine finally made her way downstairs. He rose at her entrance, and surveyed her with a frankly approving smile.

"Now, it's understood," said Frances, as she saw them to the door, "that you are to return in time for luncheon, so I shall look to see you no later."

"Your chaperone evidently doesn't care to trust you too long in my company," remarked Crendon, as he handed Catherine up into the curricle which was awaiting them outside in the care of a groom.

He swung himself up into the vehicle after her, and took up the reins, dismissing the groom with a nod.

"If she does not, you have only yourself to blame, sir," she answered, with a saucy look.

"Very true." His dark eyes lingered on her face. "And I'm sure she is wise. You look so delectable this morning, a more prudent man than myself would be hard put to it to keep the line."

Catherine was delighted with this remark, but she knew better than to take it seriously.

"I dare say you say exactly the same thing to all the ladies you take out driving with you," she said, laughing.

"To be sure I do. It's expected of a man, after all. But I don't always mean it as much as I do at the present moment."

She found his candour refreshing, though at times it took her aback. This morning, it added exactly the right touch of piquancy to what was a delightful occasion. The curricle bowled merrily over the road which ran along the white cliffs, with the sea far below sparkling in the bright sunshine. A little breeze, just enough to prevent the weather from being too hot, set the ribbons of her bonnet fluttering. She was in a mood to be pleased, and kept up a constant flow of happy chatter.

After they had driven about four miles, they turned inland to reach Rottingdean, a pleasant village grouped about a green. Here Crendon reined in the horses so that they could survey the scene. The old village church rose above a pond on which ducks sailed serenely, flirting their tails or submerging in a flurry from time to time in search of food. Close by on the path a man stood motionless, gazing across the pond abstractedly, as though lulled by the peace and beauty surrounding him.

Catherine glanced incuriously at him, then started violently, and looked again, this time more intently.

"Well I'm blessed!" she exclaimed, excitedly. "If it isn't Oliver! Oh, Captain Crendon, I must speak to him — pray set me down for a moment!"

The man heard her voice and looked up. After a brief hesitation, he walked round the path towards them and stopped beside the curricle.

"Ka— Miss Catherine," he said, removing his hat and bowing. "I did not think to see you here, so far from your home — it is indeed a surprise."

"Not such a surprise as it is to me to see *you* here, Oliver, for you must recall that we were promised to my sister Fanny in Brighton this age past. But I am forgetting —" turning to her companion — "you two do not know each other. Oliver, this is Captain Crendon — Captain, this is Mr. Seaton, whom my family have known for ever. We are neighbours at home."

The gentlemen acknowledged the introduction with bows, and ventured a few polite remarks about the weather.

"But I must have a word with Oliver in private, if you will forgive me, Captain Crendon, for I have something of the utmost urgency to say to him. If you will be good enough to hand me down, and wait just a few minutes —"

The Captain shrugged. "As you wish, ma'am. But I never knew a woman yet who could say anything, however urgent, in a few minutes; and as these beasts of mine are still frisky, and won't take kindly to standing, I propose to tool them around a bit, and pick you up later. Shall we say in a quarter of an hour? How will that suit?"

"But, Katie," began Oliver Seaton, hesitantly, "do you think we should —"

His glance fell on Crendon, who was eyeing him curiously, and he said no more, but reached up his hand to Catherine to help her dismount from the curricle. In this he managed to forestall the Captain, who had been about to jump down, but who now resumed his seat with a faintly disgruntled air.

"As you are neighbours," he said, as he once more took up the reins, "I imagine Mrs. Hailsham can have no possible objection to my leaving you in Mr. Seaton's care for a short time." He nodded casually. "I will return here for you in a quarter hour, then."

He wheeled, and disappeared down the lane in a cloud of dust. Catherine looked after him and laughed.

"I do believe he was put out at my wanting to speak with you! How absurd!"

"Who is the fellow?" asked Oliver, forgetting his new role and falling into the old childhood one of playmate and protector. "Is he a particular friend of yours, Katie?"

"He's one of John's officers. Why, no, not to say particular — I only met him a few days since."

"Then I wonder that Fanny permits you to go gallivanting round the countryside with him," he said, sternly.

"Oh, fiddle! Fanny says it's quite proper, so there's no need for you to concern yourself with that."

"I forgot," he replied, contritely. "I have been used in the past to advise and in some sort control all you girls, for you have no brother, and we were thrown a great deal together. But all that is changed, now, of course; you are all grown up, and I haven't the smallest right —"

"Oh, stuff and nonsense!" exclaimed Catherine, with more emphasis than elegance. "Don't be so — so confoundedly *humble*, Oliver! It quite sickens me, when I think what an autocrat you used to be when we were in the nursery!"

"Humility is —"

"I know, yes," she cut in, impatiently. "You are about to inform me that it is a Christian virtue. Only pray do not, Oliver, or I shall scream! I'm not sure, you know," she added, reflectively, "that I could ever marry a clergyman."

He grinned. "Well, if it's any consolation to you, I may say that I'm quite sure you should not do so. The good ladies of the parish might find you a little disconcerting, to say the least. But I'm sure you didn't want to talk to me about that. Didn't you say there was something urgent?"

"Well, yes, naturally I said that, for Captain Crendon's benefit. Actually, I thought *you* might wish to talk to *me* — to ask me how Louisa did, I mean."

A change came over his face. "You are quite right; the moment I saw you, I wanted to ask after her, even though I know very well I should not."

"I don't see why not," remarked Catherine, puzzled.

"After the promise we made to your parents? A promise which —" he sighed heavily — "has already been broken once."

"Oh, what rubbish you do talk, Oliver!" she exclaimed, in disgust. "Accidental meetings are bound to occur — and, anyway, you didn't promise never to speak to me, or Nell, or any of the rest of us!"

"You could say so; and yet if I use meetings with the rest of you to glean news of —" his voice faltered for a moment — "of Louisa, I am not keeping the spirit of my promise."

"Oh, well, if you're determined to be so noble, I have nothing to say to you!" replied Catherine, in a huff. "Lou told us that you'd said she was to do her best to forget you. She was making wretched enough work of it at first, but I may as well tell you that she made some headway yesterday evening, at the Grand Rose Ball!"

She was sorry the moment she had said it. A change came at once over Oliver's face; it was as though the sun had suddenly been overcast with heavy cloud.

"What do you mean?" he asked, in a strangled voice.

"Oh, nothing! I — I was being spiteful, I suppose," she answered with reluctant honesty. "You do so vex me when you persist in being high-minded all the time."

"That I perfectly understand — it was always so when we were children. But there was something in what you said — some underlying truth — I know; it was not simply retaliation."

Catherine shrugged. "Oh, nothing but that Lou danced with somebody else for the first time in I don't know how many months. And why should she not? We have all been nagging at her to come out of the vapours and try to enjoy herself a little."

"May I ask who was the man?" he said, quietly.

"Oh — Viscount Pamyngton. It was only civil, you know," she added, hastily, "that he should ask us to dance, for Lady Nevern and Mama are such old friends. He danced with

Fanny, too, later on; and he asked me, though I was not disengaged at the time."

He was silent for a moment. Catherine watched him uneasily.

"Pamyngton," he said at last, heavily. "Yes, I know that your parents have long desired a match with him for one of you girls."

"Now, pray don't be jumping to conclusions, Oliver! As a matter of fact, Lord Pamyngton has been paying attentions to me, not to Lou — that is, as far as he can be truly said to have paid anyone serious attentions at all. He is merely amusing himself."

She saw at once that this was quite the wrong thing to have said. A deep frown darkened Oliver's face.

"Amusing himself, is he?" he said, grimly. "We'll see about that! If another man — one more eligible in a worldly sense than I — were to find favour in Louisa's eyes, then perforce I must give up all thought of her. But only if that man can offer her a true, steadfast devotion such as I — poor wretch that I am — feel for her! If any man seeks to amuse —" his voice trembled with anger — "amuse himself with a girl who is as far above — but never mind about that! Depend on it, he will have me to reckon with!"

Catherine clapped her hands. "Oh, bravo, Oliver! How I love you when you are unchristian!"

He gave a reluctant smile. "At times you're a minx, young woman."

"So Fanny says. But one cannot be serious all the time."

"No, and we all realize the good qualities that underlie that frivolous exterior of yours."

"Well, I'm glad you think so, at any rate, though I'm far from certain of it myself. But no matter. Would you like me to take some message to Lou?"

He shook his head. "I must not do that, sorely as I am tempted. And I think it will be better, Katie, if you say nothing of this meeting today. The only thing is —"

He broke off, frowning.

"Yes, what?" she prompted him, impatiently. "We haven't very long now, Oliver. Captain Crendon will soon be back, and I mustn't keep him waiting."

He pulled out his watch and stared at it, still frowning. "Yes, you are right. There's only one thing, Katie; one service you could render me, if you would."

"Anything, of course. Just say what it is."

"I would like further news of how this man Pamyngton conducts himself towards Louisa. Do you suppose that you and I could meet again from time to time?"

"But where?" she asked, helplessly. "You can't come to West Street, and I can't come here very often. By the way, Oliver, what are you doing here in the first place? I forgot to ask you that."

"I have a post as tutor here at the Vicarage," he explained, briefly. "I took it thinking to set a distance between Louisa and myself — you see with what result. But as to where we can meet, now —"

He paused to consider this point, while Catherine waited, now and then glancing along the road to see if there was any sign of Crendon's curricle. At last Oliver Seaton seemed to arrive at a decision.

"I cannot come to you in Brighton, for any meeting place there would be too public. The only thing, then, is for you to come here to me. It's a quiet place, and we're unlikely to be observed by anyone who knows us. I will hire a hackney and give the jarvey instructions to pick you up somewhere not too far from your sister's house — say outside the Ship Inn, on the sea front. But how to decide a day and hour that will be convenient for us both? I must confess that puzzles me. The best time for me is the evening, for then I am free from my duties; but I dare say that is the busiest time of day for you, in the bustle of a Brighton season."

"Oh, I dare say I could contrive something, if you are set on it. But I assure you, Oliver, there is no need. Lord Pamyngton does not show any undue interest in Lou, nor she in him. There's nothing but civility between them, upon my word. I was but talking foolishly — you know very well how it is with me when you put my back up!"

"Indeed I do, Katie, but I cannot feel entirely easy now that you've put the notion into my head. I know it's asking a great deal of you, and perhaps it is wrong of me to persuade you to a course of what is, after all, deception —"

"Oh, if you're to moralize again, I have done!" exclaimed Catherine, in disgust. "For my part, I think it would be a splendid lark! Yes, I will meet you, by all means, but do not send for me, for how will you know if I can manage to come? It would be best, perhaps, for you to be here at a fixed time — say between eight and nine o'clock in the evening — and for me to come if I am able. I can take a hackney myself from the stand in North Street, which is only a step from Fanny's. And if I don't arrive by nine o'clock, you will know I couldn't get away. How will that be? Now, how often will you want me to come? And don't say every day, for that would be impossible, besides being a great waste of time!"

They had just settled to try and meet on that day week, when the sound of carriage wheels and hoofs invaded their peace, and the curricle drew up beside the village green.

Chapter XI: Ditched

"I trust you enjoyed your little chat," remarked Crendon, with studied politeness, as he turned the curricle homewards.

"Well, yes — that is to say, I was glad to have an opportunity of talking to Oliver. It was very good of you to wait for me. I do hope you did not find it too much of a bore."

"Not at all," he replied, in a sarcastic tone. "I am never bored when I drive out with a pretty woman, even if she does leave me for another beau."

She laughed. "Oliver's no beau of mine, Captain Crendon."

"What, did you use the time to quarrel with him? What a waste of an opportunity!"

"No, I assure you," she protested. "Oliver Seaton means nothing to me, nor I to him. He's in love with my sister Louisa, on the contrary; but my parents won't consent to their marriage."

"Is the fellow a rake, or something?" he asked, carelessly.

"Good gracious! Oliver! Why, he's a clergyman!"

"What has that to say to anything?"

She regarded him uncertainly for a moment, then gave a reluctant laugh. "I suppose you're in jest again. No, you see the trouble is that Oliver has only a small income and no expectations that one knows of so my parents think him unsuitable as a husband, while liking and respecting him as a man."

"What about your sister? Has she not some means on which they could live?"

"Oh, yes," replied Catherine, surprised. "She is well provided for, as, indeed, we all are. But you see, that only makes things worse from Oliver's point of view."

"How so? If she has money enough for both they may wed without your parents' blessing. That is, unless they have the power to cut your sister off from her fortune."

Catherine shook her head. "No. It is arranged so that our fortune goes with us when we marry. But that isn't the point — Oliver's not the man to live on his wife's money. Unless he was in possession of an income which matched hers, he would feel that he was nothing better than a fortune-hunter."

"What's so wrong with that? Fortune-hunting without love may be a reprehensible thing, perhaps; but where there exists an equal amount of affection between the two parties, what matters it which has the money?"

"You can't truly think so," Catherine protested. "Everyone despises a fortune-hunter — that much you must acknowledge."

"Devil a bit," he replied, with a laugh. "Those who chance to be on the lookout for a means of repairing their own pockets will never despise a successful fortune-hunter. On the contrary, they envy him for having brought off what they would give quite a few years of their life-span to achieve."

"I must tell you, Captain Crendon," she said, in a distant tone, "that you have some very odd notions of which I don't altogether approve."

"What you mean, my dear Miss Catherine, is that I never scruple to say outright what most people are at pains to conceal. But let us leave the subject, since evidently we can't agree. You shall think your Mr. Seaton a paragon, and I will continue to consider him a slow-top. How will that do?"

She relaxed into a smile. "Oh, well I must confess that I did have something the same notion of him, though not for the same reasons. But I see now I was wrong — he has not completely abandoned all hope of winning my sister. We have engaged in a little conspiracy, he and I." She assumed an air of mystery.

"I ought not to ask you about it, I know," he said, sarcastically, "but you are so evidently longing to tell me, that I see no point in further subterfuge. Pray do unburden yourself, Miss Catherine, and I vow to be as silent as the proverbial grave."

"How horridly you do put things!" she exclaimed, pouting. "Just for that, I shall not tell you."

"As you please," he replied, indifferently.

There was a piqued silence on her part that lasted several minutes. But he had not been wrong in thinking that she was bursting to confide her secret. Presently she looked at him out of the corner of her eye and said provocatively, "We have arranged to meet secretly in Rottingdean from time to time, so that I may tell him how Louisa goes on."

"Have you now? But wouldn't it be simpler for the fellow to ride over to Brighton and see for himself?"

"He can't do that. You must know that he promised Mama and Papa that he wouldn't try to see Lou again."

"Very noble," he commented, with a sneer.

"Yes, it is!" flared Catherine. "Because he loves her to distraction, which is something you could never understand, I am sure!"

"Don't be so certain." He turned an intense look on her which caused a slight flutter of her pulse. "But how do you propose to get to Rottingdean without your family knowing?"

"Oh, I shall think of some excuse, then creep out and take a hackney carriage."

"To arrive at your destination covered in wisps of straw and battered half to death by a ride on broken springs?" he asked, amused. "Come, you can do better than that. I will engage to convey you there myself."

"No, would you really?" exclaimed Catherine, eagerly. "How very kind of you! I am to go today week, between eight and nine o'clock in the evening. Could you manage that, do you think, sir? I must not put you to any inconvenience, though," she added, suddenly remembering her manners.

"Have no fear; I'm not the man to put myself out unless I've a mind to do so. Yes, I think it can be arranged — we'll speak of it again, nearer the time."

Catherine began a delighted and slightly incoherent speech of thanks; then broke off to ask where they were going, as Crendon had that moment turned the curricle inland from the coast road.

"We have time and to spare, so I intend to take an inland route back, for a change," he explained.

"As long as we aren't back any later than one o'clock," said Catherine, dubiously. "I mustn't put Fanny in a taking, you know, or she may not agree to my driving out with you again, and then where would our little scheme be?"

"Be easy; the horses have plenty of go in 'em yet," he scoffed. "Hold tight, and I'll show you their paces!"

He dropped his hands, and the curricle shot forward so suddenly that Catherine was hard put to it to keep her seat. She gasped as the hedges flew past. The lane was both narrow and rough, and the curricle rocked from side to side as it jolted over potholes and huge, jagged stones, throwing up a thick cloud of dust as it went.

"Oh, stop, stop!" she gasped, clinging on to the side of the vehicle.

He laughed aloud. "Never say you're scared!"

She darted a frightened glance at his face. It wore a look of exhilaration, and his eyes glittered almost as though, Catherine thought, he was wine-taken. It crossed her mind that he might have passed the time at an inn while he was waiting for her. The thought did nothing to reassure her.

"Ye-es, I — I — am!" she managed to gasp, physical vibration combining with fright to make her stutter. "Pray do — do — stop — please —"

Her words were cut off abruptly, and the next moment she was hurled forward so that she almost fell from the carriage. Her hold on the side saved her, however, though the jerk hurt her wrists. For a moment, she felt in a daze.

Presently, she became conscious that the curricle had stopped and her companion was swearing aloud at some length, without once repeating himself. She slid back into her seat, exhausted, and realized that the vehicle had developed a dangerous list. She moistened her lips, and asked in a trembling voice what had happened.

"Damned near wrenched off a wheel and ditched into the bargain, that's what happened, God damme!" he growled. "Hold tight, will you; I'm getting down."

He sprang from the lop-sided vehicle, and made a brief inspection before going to the heads of the fidgeting horses.

"Devil a thing I can do with that," he said, scowling. "Needs a blacksmith, and the nearest's a good three miles off. Hope you're fond of walking."

"But — but —" stammered Catherine, not yet fully recovered — "how far are we from home?"

"A little matter of four or five miles, ma'am," he replied, acidly.

"But what are we to do?" she asked, plaintively. "I can't walk that distance in these shoes — and it's so hot — and, oh, I'll be dreadfully late, and Fanny will be nearly frantic —"

He muttered under his breath some suggestion concerning Fanny which luckily Catherine could not catch.

"Can you ride?" he asked. "Here's a horse apiece, though I fear I can't supply you with a lady's saddle."

"Ride?" she almost shrieked. "Ride one of those frisky, high-stepping animals? Not for anything!"

He shrugged. "As you wish. I fear, then, that there is no alternative —"

He broke off as he heard another vehicle approaching by the way they had just travelled. In a few moments, a smart yellow curricle appeared, drawn by a pair of bay horses. The driver of the vehicle drew up immediately behind them; seeing their predicament, he passed the reins to a young groom who sat beside him, and, leaping down from the curricle, came to Crendon's side.

'Ditched?" he asked, sympathetically. "Anything I can do?"

At the sound of his voice, Catherine started and turned her head away.

"Very civil of you, sir," began Crendon, then broke off as he recognized the newcomer. "But it's Viscount Pamyngton, isn't it? We met the other day — Crendon's my name, Captain Crendon, in case you've forgotten."

Pamyngton nodded. "Yes, I recollect. Deuced uncomfortable business, this, what? Shall I give you a hand to get your vehicle back on the road?"

Crendon grimaced in disgust. "No good, I fear. Wheel's fairly wrenched off — another tug will finish the job. Best left where it is until I can get a blacksmith to it. The horses are all right, thank God."

"Glad to hear it. I trust you and your lady passenger —" with a quick glance at Catherine, who still kept her head turned away — "were also fortunate enough to escape injury?"

"Oh, yes. A trifle of shock, possibly, in Miss Denham's case, but nothing to signify."

Pamyngton removed his hat, and bowed in Catherine's direction. "I thought I recognized Miss Catherine Denham," he said, and she was certain that she could detect amusement in his voice. "Can I be of any service, Captain Crendon? Possibly I could convey the lady home, and leave a message for you at the nearest smithy?"

"That might well be best," said Crendon, slowly. "We were debating when you arrived on the scene whether Miss Catherine might manage to ride one of my horses, but she did not seem at all eager to make the attempt."

"Naturally not," replied Pamyngton, with a gravity which Catherine knew very well was assumed. "Miss Catherine has already informed me that she does not care for equestrian exercise."

"No?" asked Crendon, shooting a look at Catherine. "Oh, well, it would have been difficult enough, anyway, without a lady's saddle. What do you say, Miss Catherine? Are you willing to accept Lord Pamyngton's offer of a lift back to Brighton?"

Catherine had no choice but to turn her head and reply, though her answer bordered on the ungracious.

"There seems no help for it. After all, I can't stay here for ever, can I? Before long, my sister will be getting anxious about me, too. Oh, why did you have to drive so fast? I begged you not to!"

He shrugged. "No use crying over spilt milk. You'd best get down this side — careful how you come, now."

The vehicle was certainly tilted at an alarming angle. Catherine moved cautiously over to the driver's side, and put a tentative foot out towards the step, which was several feet higher than usual from the ground. The movement started the horses fidgeting again, and Crendon left Catherine to go to their heads.

Pamyngton looked up beyond the trim ankle waving about somewhere in the region of his neckcloth, to the anxious face of its owner. He raised his arms.

"If you will permit me," he said, as he took her lightly by the waist and lifted her to the ground.

Catherine blushed, although he released her instantly and with the gentlest of touches on her arm, guided her to his own vehicle. The groom had already leapt down, and Pamyngton handed Catherine up solicitously before settling himself beside her. A nod of the head sent the groom to the perch behind them, and Pamyngton took up the reins.

"Can you get by?" asked Crendon.

Pamyngton nodded, measuring the distance with his eye. With consummate skill, he guided the curricle past the ditched vehicle with barely an inch to spare. Catherine let out a gasp of relief.

"I never thought we should do it without scraping the side!"

He smiled indulgently, and raised his hand in salute to Crendon, who replied by removing his hat and waving it in cheery fashion at Catherine.

"How did it happen?" asked Pamyngton, as they continued down the lane.

"Oh, he was driving neck or nothing," she replied, in disgust. "I begged him to desist, but he would not take the slightest heed! I really feel it served him right!"

"I collect you were anxious to reach home again."

"That wasn't the reason why he decided to spring his horses, I can assure you. I don't believe he has the slightest regard for other people's anxieties at all. He is the most selfish kind of man!"

"I am reassured to see," remarked Pamyngton, with a smile, "that you are no better pleased with him than you are with me."

"Well, no, for I consider he served me shabbily!" she retorted. "And then to suggest that I should either walk or — or ride one of those odiously high-spirited horses!"

"It was not very gallant, certainly. He ought at least to have offered to carry you himself."

She turned a smouldering look on him. "I might have known you would find it amusing!" she said, scathingly. "I wonder why it is that Fate decrees you should always be the one to come along when I am in some silly fix or other? I don't mind telling you I had far rather have someone else come to my assistance!"

"Anyone in particular?" he queried, raising an inquisitive eyebrow. "Or is your meaning that almost anyone would be preferable to myself?"

"The latter!" she snapped, quite out of temper.

He sighed gently. "Ah, dear, I feared that. You seem to have a very unforgiving nature, ma'am."

"Well, perhaps I have. I am not so angelic as my sister Louisa," she said, with meaning.

He looked at her thoughtfully, for a moment. "Now what can I possibly say to that?" he demanded, in mock dismay. "If

I disagree with you, you will accuse me, I know, of insincerity; while if I agree, you will be justifiably incensed. At such times, a sensible man should say nothing."

At that she burst out laughing, restored to her usual good humour. "Oh, you are absurd, sir! Do you mean to say nothing for the rest of our journey home, then?"

"Willingly, if it would restore me to your good books," he replied, smiling.

Catherine reflected suddenly how much Lord Pamyngton could manage to convey with one of his smiles. He could use them to flatter, tease, admonish or, as now, to express regret; but whatever the mood, there was always an underlying gentleness which could not give offence. She remembered what Louisa had said about him earlier that morning, and grew silent.

"You don't answer," he said, after a moment. "They do say that silence is golden, but I am inclined to think my good fortune depends on your words."

"I was thinking," she replied, with an air of abstraction.

"Whether to forgive me or not? And what, may I venture to ask, is the verdict? Behold me in fear and trembling."

"Nothing of the kind!" laughed Catherine. "And I'm very thankful you're not, for you would not manage these horses so well if you were; and I've had quite enough of a shaking-up for one day, I can tell you."

"That I can believe." He glanced at her solicitously. "You were not hurt at all, I trust? I should have asked you before, but that Crendon seemed to dismiss the subject airily enough, and you yourself made no complaint."

"No, I suffered no injury. As for the Captain, he would dismiss anything airily, I feel sure."

"That commends itself to you?"

She shrugged. "Not particularly. Why should you think so?"

He hesitated. "You consented to dance with him yesterday evening, and went driving with him this morning. He was favoured above myself, so naturally I assumed that you found his style more congenial."

"He's amusing," she said, consideringly. "And certainly not just in the style of most gentlemen one meets."

"While I am." He bowed ironically. "I see I must study to be different."

"You don't need to do so." she said, with her usual frankness. "You are not like Captain Crendon, but you have a style that is all your own. My sister was remarking on it this morning."

"Mrs. Hailsham? Or one of your other sisters?" he queried.

"It was Lou — that is, my sister Louisa."

'She is a charming young lady, and not, I think, very happy just at present," he remarked, quietly.

"No. You may remember I told you about that when —" she hesitated, and coloured a little — "when we first met."

He pretended not to have noticed her slight confusion. "Yes, I do recollect. You said she had fallen in love with someone unsuitable, and your parents had forbidden the match. Can there be no hope for them?"

"Not that anyone can see. Oliver Seaton is a clergyman and well liked personally by my parents — we've known his family all our lives — but his living will be a meagre one, and there is no prospect of advancement for him. He has told Lou that she must try and forget him, and somehow one can't help feeling it's the sensible thing to do, though quite odiously unromantic, of course."

He was silent for a moment, then said, "It's not easy to forget a strong attachment."

"No, and although Oliver says it, he does not practise what he preaches, for only this morning I saw him, and he asked me to keep him informed of how Lou goes on —"

"This Mr. Seaton is staying in Brighton?" he asked, in surprise.

"Oh, no," she exclaimed, alarmed at her indiscretion, "and please you are to say nothing to Lou of my meeting him! It was quite by chance. I did not know — none of us did — that he had taken a post as tutor in Rottingdean until his living falls vacant; and it was such a surprise to see him there when Captain Crendon and I drove into the village. I have promised to meet him sometimes, and the Captain has undertaken to drive me there for the purpose." She paused, frowning. "I did not wish to let the Captain into the secret, but I was obliged to explain why I wished to be private with Oliver for a while. He — Captain Crendon — thought Oliver was one of my beaux! Imagine!"

"A natural enough assumption. You certainly did not lack for partners last night," he said, smiling. Then, in a more serious tone — "I collect that you think it wiser for your sister not to know that this gentleman is so close at hand?"

"Well, you see, they have given their word that they will neither meet nor correspond. Oliver did not know that we were to come to Brighton, or no doubt he would have found a post elsewhere."

"One feels for them," he said, sincerely.

"Yes, indeed." She was pensive for a while, then burst out — "If only I could think of something to do that would help! And the stupid thing is, as I was telling Captain Crendon, that Lou has an easy competence of her own that would be more than enough for them to live on, without Oliver needing to possess a penny. Only that will not do for Oliver, of course." She paused, then turned impulsively towards him. "What do you think, Lord Pamyngton? Do you believe that it's of no account who has the fortune, so long as there is affection between two people?"

He pursed his lips and pondered for a while. "I do, in theory," he answered, eventually, "but not, I fear, in practice. I should not care to feel that I was living on my wife — in short I would prefer not to marry a woman of greater fortune than myself."

She nodded, satisfied. "Yes, I am confident that most gentlemen would think as you do. But Captain Crendon does not, I must tell you. He says that there is no harm at all in fortune-hunting where there is also affection."

"He has the reputation of being a — somewhat unorthodox man," he said, mildly. "And he may have been in jest, you know."

"I am not such a cloth-head that I don't realize when someone is joking me!" she exclaimed, with feigned indignation.

"Oh, dear! I fear I have offended you again. It is, of course, none of my business; and you must not hesitate to say so if you feel I am exceeding the bounds of our uncertain — dare I say friendship? But do you think your sister, Mrs. Hailsham, is at all likely to permit you to take the frequent drives to Rottingdean with Crendon, which will no doubt be necessary if you are to keep your clergyman friend informed in this way?"

"No, she certainly would not, and especially not at the hour when Oliver is able to meet me, which is between eight and nine o'clock in the evening. I shall be obliged to slip away in secret," she said, with a certain relish, "and contrive to send a message to Captain Crendon to pick me up somewhere or other. It will be prodigious fun, don't you think?"

"Undoubtedly." His tone was dry. "But — forgive me — perhaps not very wise? You are placing a great deal of trust in Crendon, whom you have not known very long, after all."

"Long enough to discover that we are the same kind of people," she replied, tartly. "Anyway, as you said yourself, it is no business of yours. After all, I haven't known you very long, either — and at least the Captain did not try to deceive me about his name!"

He said no more. She stole a look at his face, and saw that it was grave, with the lips set in a hard line. She had never seen him look like this before, and did not like it. All at once, her strongest wish was to see him smiling again. She placed her hand on his arm in an impulsive, almost childlike gesture.

"I'm a nagging wretch," she said, contritely, "and ungrateful, too, for you've come to my rescue countless times. Come, we'll quarrel no more."

His hand came out to cover hers for a brief moment. She coloured and quickly drew her own away.

"Willingly," he said, quietly, giving her one short, serious look.

Then he turned his attention to the road ahead, and chatted light-heartedly on trivial matters until they reached the house in West Street.

Chapter XII: An Excursion to Devil's Dyke

The Denhams had their first glimpse of Mrs. Fitzherbert a few days later, when they were walking to Donaldson's library. She was sitting with the Prince of Wales on the iron-work balcony of her house, in full view of the crowds strolling up and down the Steyne.

"They often sit there together," remarked Colonel Hailsham. "In fact, there are those who will have it that there's a secret underground passage between the house and the Pavilion, as Prinney usually does not part from the lady until late at night in his own house, and yet is often on view seated on the balcony at hers soon after breakfast the next morning."

In view of his audience, he refrained from adding that there could be a more simple explanation of this.

"They are both very fat," said Eleanor, in disgust.

"Yes, but she is attractive in a way, don't you think?" asked Frances. "For a woman of fifty, I mean?"

"Her colouring's so pretty," declared Catherine, after a discreet look. "It's like yours, Lou, but, of course, without the appeal of youth. She's like a slightly overblown rose."

"Are they really and truly married?" asked Eleanor in a hushed voice.

"Legally, no," replied the Colonel, in a similarly low tone. "But there was a valid religious ceremony, which is recognized by the Pope. For Mrs. Fitzherbert is of the Catholic faith," he added, in explanation.

"Then," said Louisa, firmly, "she is the true wife of the Prince of Wales."

"That's as may be," put in Frances, "but at any rate she's treated almost like a Queen here in Brighton. They may not quite go so far as to 'Highness' her in the domestic circle; but they 'Madam' her prodigiously, and stand up longer for her arrival than they do for most other people."

"Almost the only person who doesn't accord her a near Royal respect is George Brummell," remarked the Colonel. "She shows her dislike of him, too, for it, although he's by far the best influence on Prinney of anyone in his intimate circle, as she knows very well."

"Oh, you mean Beau Brummell?" asked Catherine, with interest. "I saw him once, when we were in London last year. I'd heard that he was the arbiter of male fashion, and imagine my surprise to find him quietly, almost soberly, dressed compared to some of the other gentlemen! I must admit though," she added, "that there was an air of great elegance about him."

John Hailsham laughed. "There would be. A man who won't hesitate to return a coat to his tailor for the most trifling fault, and who will spend a whole morning on the tying of a cravat, should at least be able to achieve an air of elegance."

"For my part," scoffed Eleanor, "I think such dandyism absurd! Oh, look, Katie, there is Captain Crendon coming out of Raggett's Club, and Captain North with him. I must say —" she added, smiling across at the two officers, who bowed on recognizing the Colonel's party — "that Captain Crendon doesn't look very cheerful."

"No more would you," said John Hailsham, in a low tone, as he replied to the officers' salutations, "if you were in low water, as he is at present. I heard the young fool dropped a cool five thousand at play the other evening, not for the first time. I'm not quite sure how he's placed, but few men can afford a run of that kind of luck."

"Ought you not to speak to him, John?" asked Frances. "After all, he is one of your junior officers, and you are in some sort responsible for him."

"He's scarce likely to thank me for interfering," replied the Colonel, dryly. "He's not a green 'un, my love — he's eight and twenty, and more up to snuff than most of 'em. Now, if it had been young North —" He broke off as they turned into the doorway of Donaldson's library, and paused to chat with some of his acquaintances who were gathered there.

Eleanor declared her intention of sitting down to a game of Loo, which was one of the many diversions offered by the library. She managed to persuade Frances, who was very fond of the game, to join her; but Louisa and Catherine refused, preferring to wander round the bookshelves and search out the latest novels.

They soon drew some distance apart. Catherine had picked a book entitled *Adeline Mowbray*, by a Mrs. Opie, from the shelves, and was perusing the opening chapter earnestly, when a voice at her elbow made her jump. Turning, she saw Pamyngton standing there.

"Don't let me interrupt you," he said, with a deprecating smile. "I could not pass you by without enquiring if you had quite recovered from your shaking up of the other day."

Catherine closed the book and replaced it on the shelf. "Yes, indeed, thank you." She turned to him with an answering smile. "It was nothing — though I'm most grateful to you for bringing me home. I believe I did not thank you properly at the time, being in a rush to present myself to Fanny before she went off into hysterics."

"That I don't credit — Mrs. Hailsham is made of sterner stuff, like yourself, Miss Catherine."

"Me?" she queried, ungrammatically. "You must be flattering — you can't really believe that I'm much of a heroine, when you know only too well how nervous I am with horses!"

"We all have our Achilles' heel," he replied, with a twinkle in his eye. "But you are certainly not without strength of purpose, or resourcefulness. I recall, on the occasion of our first meeting — indeed, how could I possibly forget any circumstance of that occasion?" He broke off, as he saw a faint cloud of embarrassment dim the pert brightness of her face, and continued smoothly — "But that is by the way. What I particularly wished to recall to you was the quick-witted way in which you simulated a fainting fit when every other resource had failed you."

"You are very good to say so," said Catherine, recovering. "But any fool of a girl can pretend to faint. You must realize we do it all the time, when things aren't going well."

"Do you, indeed? How very reprehensible," he said, reproachfully. "And I had not the least idea of it, of course."

She gave him a saucy look. "You are a great humbug, my lord. Do you know that?"

"Not 'my lord'," he pleaded, shaking his head. "Can you not call me Pamyngton?" He hesitated a moment, then added, "My closest friends call me Pam. It's not perhaps an attractive name, but endeared to me now by long usage. I make you free of it — willingly — if you will honour me by using it."

"But whatever will people say?" demanded Catherine, a little nonplussed by his unusually earnest manner. "I — we — have not known you long — it would not be at all proper, I am sure!"

"I am not suggesting that you should use my name before company, necessarily, but merely when we are talking tête-à-tête, as now," he said, quietly. "Besides, our parents have been close friends for years. Surely that should make some difference?"

Her face cleared, and the familiar impish look which so delighted him appeared once more.

"Oh, well, in private, why not?" she returned, airily. "And I suppose there's no very good reason why you should be for ever calling me 'Miss Catherine' or 'ma'am'. In return, you may call me Katie, as my family do — though not within my brother-in-law's hearing, I beg you, for he's a stickler for convention, and especially where we girls are concerned, I may tell you!"

"Very proper: he is, after all, responsible for you while you are under his roof. You need have no fear that I shall abuse what I regard as a very great privilege — an honour beyond my desserts —" He broke off, his quick perception warning him that she was embarrassed by his serious manner.

"I am quite in despair," he said, in a lighter tone, "of ever finding any flowers hereabouts which you would care to receive. Would you believe it, the wretched flower-sellers have nothing which is out of season? However, if you will favour me with a list of those you most fancy, I will send to the farthest corners of the earth to try and obtain them."

She gave a little gurgle of laughter. "Oh, you are so absurd, my l— I mean, Pam."

The name came out diffidently, with a shy glance from her unusual, gold-flecked eyes that brought a quick leap to his pulse.

His manner was calm, however, as he said, "I've been wondering if I could persuade you young ladies to join an expedition to Devil's Dyke, which is planned for this afternoon. A number of people whom you've already met are going — young Eversley, Fullerton and his sisters, one or two of the officers and their ladies —"

"Captain Crendon?" asked Catherine, quickly.

He looked at her intently for a moment, then shook his head. "No, Crendon is not one of our party. If you would like him to be included, however —"

"Oh, no, it's of no account. I just wondered, when you mentioned some officers."

"Major Drummond and Captain Mostyn," he explained. "Their wives first put forward the suggestion the other evening at the ball, and your sister Eleanor was quite enthusiastic about it. Has she said nothing to you?"

"Why, yes, I think she did; but Nell has so many enthusiasms! She has been pestering Fanny the last day or two to let her go to the fair on White Hawk Down, but Fanny says it's not at all the thing, because it attracts such a tatterdemalion crowd, full of pickpockets and other desperate characters."

"Mrs. Hailsham is quite right, of course; though I can understand the attraction of a fairground for a lively young lady like Miss Eleanor."

"Well, yes, it might be fun, don't you think? I would dearly love," said Catherine, with sparkling eyes "to have my fortune told by a gipsy!"

He laughed. "Would you? I am tempted to dash out and pull one in by the hair — except of course, that I am somewhat put off by the thought that a gipsy's hair is unlikely to have more than a nodding acquaintance with soap and water!"

"Oh surely that cannot be so? They live by babbling brooks, and run barefoot through dewy grass —"

"Only in poetry, I fear." He shook his head in a melancholy gesture.

"I am making the humiliating discovery that gentlemen are sadly unromantic," she said, sighing.

"Ah, yes, we're a poor lot of wretches. Yet I think —" he dropped his voice to an intimate tone that brought a sudden catch in her breath — "we can summon up sufficient romance to pass muster — on an appropriate occasion, Katie."

She turned away, suddenly, taking a spurious interest in the bookshelves. "Well, you must ask Fanny, of course, if we may join the party but I think I may answer for both my sisters that we would like to come. See, there is Lou; we'll ask her now. And you'll find Fanny and Nell playing Loo in the other room. What a place Brighton is for gaming, to be sure!"

"You can scarce call it gaming in this establishment. The stakes are so low, only ladies will play."

They moved over to where Louisa was sitting, engrossed in a book. She expressed her willingness to make one of the party, and Pamyngton then sought out Frances and Eleanor. He found no difficulty in persuading Frances to agree to the plan. Everyone in the party was known to her, and there would be two married ladies present to act as chaperons and absolve her from the duty of going herself. She felt pleased that Pamyngton was to be in company with her sisters for a whole afternoon; this would be welcome news for Mama.

Eleanor was delighted with the scheme, but urged that they might return home by way of White Hawk Down, so that they could have a glimpse of the fair, if only on the outskirts. Pamyngton demurred, saying that the approaches would be very crowded, but he allowed himself to be overruled when he saw how disappointed she would be. Another slight hitch followed, over the travelling arrangements. It had been planned for the ladies to go in coaches and the men to ride; but Eleanor declared firmly that she wished to ride, too.

"Nonsense, Nell, you can't be the only female to ride alongside the gentlemen," protested Frances. "Only think how singular it would look!"

"Oh, stuff!" retorted Eleanor. "Besides, Sally Fullerton will ride with me — I know she is a very keen horsewoman. I have only to ask her."

"Oh, well, in that case. And possibly some of the other ladies will ride, too. What about her sister Jane?"

"No, she does not care for riding as much as her sister does. I don't know about Mrs. Drummond and Mrs. Mostyn, of course."

"They are firmly determined to make the journey by coach," said Pamyngton. "I had some thoughts of taking my curricle," he continued, diffidently, "in which case I could convey one of your two ladies, leaving the four others to share a coach. It would perhaps be more agreeable than splitting the party up into two coaches which must be done if there are five of you."

They all exclaimed that this was an excellent idea, but there was some difficulty about deciding whether Louisa or Catherine should accompany Pamyngton. Both girls were diffident, and clearly Pamyngton could show no preference, even if he felt any. In the end, Louisa insisted that Catherine should go.

It was a fine afternoon, and they started out in good spirits. Catherine, knowing that she looked well in her gown of soft green sarsnet, chatted gaily all the way and treated Pamyngton to more than her usual allowance of saucy looks. He responded gallantly, and at times one or two of the riding party would draw alongside to share in their effervescent conversation. Inside the carriage, too, tongues were far from silent; and Louisa, who was gradually learning to overcome the low spirits that had visited her ever since the parting from Oliver Seaton, was today as talkative as anyone else.

"What an attractive girl your sister Catherine is," remarked Mrs. Drummond, who, far from being a staid matron, was a lively woman in her late twenties. "When she smiles, she looks so impish, I'm sure all the men's heads must be turned; and in repose, her face has a great deal of sweetness. No wonder Viscount Pamyngton looks so well pleased with his present situation."

"You should never praise one woman to another, my dear Margaret," protested Mrs. Mostyn, "even if they are sisters, they take it ill."

"On the contrary," said Louisa, warmly, "I take it as a compliment to hear any member of my family praised so you may sound Katie's praises as long as you wish. And if you could also put in a good word for Nell," she added, with a smile, "I should be prodigiously flattered."

They laughed at this. "Oh, well, my dear Louisa," said Mrs. Mostyn, "you are all handsome girls there's no denying, and to my mind you're the handsomest of them all. Tell me, is it true that the Countess of Nevern once wanted your sister Fanny for her son? I have heard it said often enough."

Louisa hesitated. "I think there was some such notion, once," she said, at last. "Mama and Lady Nevern are friends of long standing."

"Then perhaps," said Mrs. Drummond, with a significant glance at the window which was meant to indicate the curricle ahead of them, "the notion need not be altogether abandoned."

Louisa was grateful to Jane Fullerton for at once changing the subject to the latest fashions; and afterwards nothing personal was touched on again.

Eleanor rode most of the way beside Frederick Eversley, who was still a favourite with her, in spite of the many young officers she had found to flirt with since coming to Brighton. Stephen Fullerton, finding it tame to ride beside his sister, occasionally broke up the jovial partnership to claim his fair share of Eleanor's sunny smiles.

The whole journey was a gradual ascent with fine views all the way, first of the sea and then of the great expanse of the Downs. At last they reached a huge, curving cleft in the hillside which Freddy Eversley announced to be the Devil's Dyke. The party continued a little farther, to the summit of the hill. Then everyone left the vehicles and horses, and stood in comparative silence to admire the view.

"Why is it called the Devil's Dyke?" asked Eleanor.

"The legend goes," explained Major Drummond, "that the devil thought people in Sussex were too pious, and so he dug this great trench with the notion of bringing in the sea to flood all the churches. He had to finish the task before dawn. An old woman held up a candle at the window of her cottage and this deceived him into thinking that the sun was up, whereupon he downed tools with the task unfinished; but he left this Dyke for us to admire."

"But surely the devil is supposed to be full of guile?" laughed Catherine. "How then did he come to be so taken in?"

"Ah, that is not explained by the legend as we know it," said Captain Mostyn. "But I think your objection very sound, Miss Catherine."

"It is so quiet up here," remarked Louisa, in a dreamy tone, "so remote. Who would believe that down there in Brighton the Steyne is at this moment crowded with people?"

"You prefer solitary places?" Pamyngton asked her, moving over to her side.

Louisa, always reluctant to express her opinions in a crowd, glanced about her. She was relieved to see that for the moment the others were talking among themselves, and paying no attention to herself and Pamyngton.

"Sometimes," she admitted.

"But more often of late, I believe?" he asked, gently.

She coloured under his kind scrutiny, and nodded. "There are times, sir, when one needs peace and quiet for reflection," she said, in a low tone.

"But not today, Miss Denham," he pleaded half in jest, half in earnest. "Not on my outing, which I had hoped would give everyone pleasure. I beg you to laugh a little today, just to please me."

She looked up at that, and for a moment he caught the likeness to Catherine as she smiled at him.

"Very well, sir — to please you," she said, lightly.

He gave a satisfied nod. When he turned towards the others, he noticed that Mrs. Mostyn's gaze was fixed upon Louisa and himself. Evidently she had been watching them with interest during their short conversation. He knew the woman had a reputation for being a gossip, and wondered wryly what capital she would make out of his dealings that afternoon with both Louisa and Catherine Denham. The thought worried him not one jot; and he rather fancied that it would not greatly concern either of the young ladies.

Chapter XIII: White Hawk Fair

The party lingered some time in the vicinity of the Dyke before starting on the homeward journey by way of the charming little Downland village of Poynings, where they stopped to refresh themselves at an inn. They then joined the turnpike road, and it was well after six o'clock before they reached the point near Brighton where they must turn off to go round by way of White Hawk Down.

Here carriages and riders halted while a brief discussion took place. Most were in favour of returning home by the shortest route; they spoke of the imminence of dinner, and the delays they were likely to meet in the crowded vicinity of the fair. Eleanor's disappointment was so outspoken, however, in spite of Louisa's frowns, that Frederick Eversley declared at once that he would go that way with her, and the rest might return straight home. Catherine and Louisa both felt that this would not do; Frances would certainly not approve of Eleanor, the youngest and flightiest of the three sisters, being left alone in such a rowdy setting with a young man whom she scarcely knew.

Seeing their doubts, Pamyngton suggested that he and Catherine should accompany the two riders. He felt Mrs. Mostyn's cynical eye upon him, and guessed that she was storing this up to add to a lurid account of his flirtations that afternoon. He reflected that one of the evils of being an eligible bachelor was that one became a constant target for gossip. It was a pity that he had been obliged to include the lady in the party, but unfortunately no man could choose the wives of his friends.

Louisa was obviously relieved at this solution to the problem. She undertook to explain everything to Frances, but begged her sisters not to be too long in following her home. Catherine promised readily enough, for she was going only to oblige Eleanor; but Eleanor waved an airy good-bye and wasting no time in words, cantered off along the road which they were to take, closely followed by Freddy Eversley.

They had still some way to go, so that the sun was setting as they approached White Hawk Down. The noise of the fair reached their ears well before they came in sight of it; as they drew nearer, they became entangled in a press of vehicles and people on foot. Catherine gazed across the heads of the noisy throng to the tents and stalls already lit by flaring torches although daylight had not yet faded, to the gaudy roundabouts and swings from which came screams of delight. A runaway pig, perhaps part of some ludicrous sideshow, charged squealing into the crowd surrounding the curricle.

Catherine watched, laughing, as it ran hither and thither, eluding all attempts to capture it. At last, it turned suddenly and scampered back by the way it had come, blundering into a girl who was carrying a bucket of water which promptly discharged itself on the yelling bystanders.

"Oh, dear!" gasped Catherine, wiping tears of mirth from her eyes, "that was one of the funniest things I've seen for a long time!"

Pamyngton agreed; then looked sharply about him for Eleanor and Freddy Eversley. So far, his attention had been divided between the antics of the pig and following the expressions on Catherine's face as she showed her uninhibited enjoyment of the scene. Now he frowned, seeing no trace of the others.

"I've lost sight of your sister and Eversley," he said. "Can you see them anywhere in the crowd?"

Reluctantly, Catherine dragged her gaze away from the pig, which was now being driven back to its base by an incensed girl with an empty bucket while the onlookers laughed and cheered.

After a few moments' scrutiny, she had to admit that she could not see their companions anywhere in the vicinity.

"Then where the devil can they have got to?" Pamyngton muttered, in some concern. "It's high time we were moving off, unless Mrs. Hailsham is to be put about by your late return."

"Why, there are their horses, tethered to that post!" exclaimed Catherine, pointing to a spot not far away, where several horses were standing. "Do you know what? I'm certain that wretched Nell has persuaded Mr. Eversley to take her on to the fair ground! I declare, it's a great deal too bad of her, for we said we mustn't stay."

He scanned the nearest booths and stalls for a while, then shook his head, frowning.

"It's no use trying to find them from here," he said, decisively, "and to go down into the crowd will take too long. I'd best convey you home. There's a man in charge of their horses, I see, and we can leave them a message with him."

"But I can't go home without Nell!" cried Catherine, in dismay. "What would Fanny say?"

"That you have done the most sensible thing, I should imagine," he said, reassuringly. "Time goes quickly to people who are enjoying themselves, and if we see them back here in half an hour, I confess I shall be surprised. No harm can come to your sister while Freddy Eversley has her in charge. You may be quite confident on that score."

"That may be so, but I had far rather stay here until she comes back," replied Catherine, obstinately. "You wouldn't understand, but I've always taken care of Nell. She's so headstrong, you know."

"While you, of course," he returned, with gentle mockery, "are never given to impetuosity."

"Oh I know you believe I am just as foolish," she told him, with a slightly shamefaced look, "and I'll admit you have some cause. But if you knew both of us really well, you would be forced to admit that Nell is even more — more heedless of danger — than I am myself."

"Very well," he conceded reluctantly. "We will wait for them, since you cannot be comfortable otherwise."

It was really no hardship to sit there in the curricle, watching the constantly changing scene before them. Catherine's eyes were drawn to a group of gipsies standing a little distance away, selling fairings to the crowd. She had a sudden impulse to jump down and ask them to read her fortune. She confided this to Pamyngton, laughing a little self-consciously.

"I dare say I could tell your fortune as well as any gipsy may," he teased her.

"Oh, could you, then?" she challenged him, with a smile. "Well, do so. Here is my palm."

She extended her hand towards him and he took the soft, white fingers in his own firm ones, looking up into her eyes.

"Your eyes are the colour of sherry wine," he said, suddenly.

She laughed. "But that is not to tell my fortune, sir! You must tell me something I do not know, such as that I will meet a tall, dark, handsome stranger — or take a journey over the water —"

"You will meet a tall, fair, very ordinary man," he interrupted, "in a most out of the ordinary way. You will be vexed with him —"

She gave him a saucy smile. "Yes? And then —?"

"He will be desolated — utterly cast down," he continued, audaciously. "You will forgive him, and he will be in transports of delight."

"Oh, you are cheating! You must tell what neither of us knows — you must forecast the future, to be a true fortune-teller!"

He shook his head sadly. "Alas, would that I could do so! I might perhaps forecast the gentleman's part in the story with reasonable accuracy; but as for your part — your future, Katie —"

His voice had changed subtly, with the last few words. She coloured a little, and snatched her hand away.

"You are no good at all as a gipsy," she said, trying to hide her confusion. "I must wait for a real one to know my fortune, I can see." Her tone changed to a more serious one. "Do you not think, sir, we should go down into the crowd in search of Nell and Mr. Eversley?"

"I will do so, if you wish; but I think you would do better to stay here. You will be jostled unmercifully in the crush."

She shrugged. "Oh, I don't regard that, I assure you. I should be glad to get down and walk for a while; I am quite tired of sitting still!"

He felt that courtesy forbade him to oppose her further. The curricle was left in charge of the man who was keeping watch over the tethered horses, and Pamyngton, not without some misgivings, guided his charge on to the fairground.

Almost at once, they were surrounded by people who were at cross-purposes to themselves; for whereas they wished to hurry on from one point to another in search of their lost companions, everyone else on the fairground seemed determined to loiter in front of every booth and sideshow. At first, Pamyngton tried to steer Catherine through the press of people by drawing her arm within his; but after a while, he found that the only way to shield her adequately from the constant jostling and pushing was to place a protective arm about her shoulders. She suffered this necessary familiarity without comment, but all the same she was conscious of it, in spite of the novelty of the occasion.

After being pushed hither and thither for a while at the whim of the crowd, they found themselves standing close to the gaily painted roundabout with its glassy-eyed horses which whirled and twisted in response to the tireless efforts of the man who cranked the mechanism.

"There's Nell!" cried Catherine, suddenly, pointing to a laughing rider on this contraption. "And Mr. Eversley, beside her! Nell! Nell!"

Her voice did not carry as far as the riders on the roundabout, but several people close at hand heard her, and stared curiously. One of them, a man with a slightly rolling gait, who was dressed in apparel that had been high fashion a few years back, came closer and gave her a long, appraising look. Then he touched his hat with a tipsy gesture.

"Haven't we met before, young lady?" he asked, familiarly. "Seems to me I know your face — and a pretty one into the bargain, if your beau there won't take the remark amiss."

Pamyngton felt Catherine shrink within the shelter of his arm. He looked down into her face, and saw that it was pale, even in the flaring light of the torches. He raised a questioning eyebrow, and she shook her head almost imperceptibly in answer.

He turned to address the speaker. "No proper compliment to a lady can come amiss," he said, smoothly, with just a faint emphasis on the second word. "But you are mistaken, sir. This lady does not know you."

"Well, now, me buck," replied the man, poking a waggish finger at Pamyngton's top waistcoat button, "I think it's you who are mistaken, for I'll warrant she knows me very well indeed if she chooses."

"I don't, nor do I wish to!" exclaimed Catherine on a slight note of hysteria.

"You heard that, I think," Pamyngton addressed the man in a clear, incisive tone very different from his normal pleasant one. "And should you require to have the matter made more plain, I would be most happy to oblige you."

The man backed a step or two at this, staggered a little, and waved his hand airily. "Not at all. I'm no spoil-sport, to come between a beau and his belle. If she don't choose to know me, let be, let be."

He turned and pushed his way back into the crowd. One or two of them had paused to listen to the interchange in the hope of seeing it come to a fight; being disappointed in this, they, too, went about their own concerns.

Pamyngton steered Catherine skilfully into a space at the back of a booth, which housed the Two-Headed Lady of the Orient, who being in reality no lady, was at that moment enjoying a tankard of ale with his neighbour, the Strong Man.

"It occurs to me," Pamyngton said, in a low tone, "that our friend was none other than that Sir Galahad who came to your assistance on the road when first you and I met."

She nodded. Her face glowed palely in the gathering shadows which were unrelieved here by the light from the torches. "Yes, he was," she whispered. "I was terrified for one awful moment that he would make some attempt to snatch me away!"

"You need have no fear on that score," he replied grimly. "All the same, I think it will be best for us to return to the curricle and await the others there. You have suffered enough buffeting for one evening."

She submitted readily enough, only pleading that they might go back by way of the roundabout, in case Eleanor should still be there. Accordingly they left their comparatively quiet spot and plunged once more into the turmoil of the crowd, Catherine within the protective shelter of her escort's arm.

They reached the roundabout just as it stopped. Pamyngton, whose height enabled him to see over the heads of most of the intervening crowd, scanned the contraption carefully.

"There they are!" he exclaimed presently. "I caught a glimpse of Eversley over in this direction."

He steered Catherine towards the roundabout as he spoke, trying to dodge people who moved back and forth with no regard for anyone's convenience but their own. It took a few moments to reach the front; when they succeeded, they saw a knot of people gathered in one particular place, where the centre of attention seemed to be a lady who was sitting in a woebegone attitude on an upturned packing case, her pretty blue riding dress trailing on the ground. A comfortable-looking woman was bending over her, offering some kind of restorative in a cup; and hovering in the background was a fashionably dressed young man who obviously wished himself elsewhere at that particular moment.

Catherine let out a little shriek. "Great heavens, it's Nell! Something is wrong with her!"

She left Pamyngton, and elbowed her way through the crowd to her sister's side.

"Nell! Whatever's amiss? Are you hurt?"

Eleanor looked up, her face drawn with pain.

"Oh, nothing to signify! Don't take on, Katie. I missed my footing getting off the roundabout, and I seem to have ricked my ankle. Only the worst of it is, I can't walk very well."

"My fault, I'm afraid," said Freddy Eversley, ruefully. "I started to help Miss Eleanor down, but wasn't quick enough."

"You mean she jumped down before you could get to her," said Catherine, perceptibly. "I know. That was the way of it, wasn't it, Nell?"

Eleanor gave a rueful grimace.

"Well, never mind that," went on Catherine, briskly. "What can't be cured must be endured, as Nurse used to say to us. You're quite sure it's nothing more serious, Nell?"

"Of course I am. And for heaven's sake get this crowd to go away, Katie," she went on, in a lowered tone. "The circus female there's been very good, bringing me a restorative and so on, but I am perfectly all right now and don't relish seeing everybody gather round me like vultures over carrion."

Catherine conveyed this to Pamyngton in a whisper. He dealt with the situation with characteristic promptness by desiring the onlookers to move away so that the injured lady might have more air. He then thanked the female who had come to Eleanor's aid, reinforcing his words with a suitable offering of money. This cleared a small area around Eleanor, and enabled the four of them to confer in comparative privacy about what was best to be done. One thing was quite clear in spite of Eleanor's brave protests; she could not be allowed to ride home.

"It's simple enough," said Catherine. "She must go in the curricle, and I will ride her horse."

"*You* ride that animal?" cried Eleanor, incredulously. "Don't be silly, Katie — it's far more spirited than Stella, and you know you can never stay on *her* for long!"

"I shall manage," declared Catherine, stoutly.

They disputed the point. Pamyngton listened in silence for a moment, much struck by the sisterly solicitude which impelled Catherine to offer to make such a sacrifice. Then he intervened.

"I think the best way out of our difficulty is for us to hire a carriage to convey both you ladies home. We shall find one at the inn, not quarter of a mile away from here." He turned to Eversley. "Freddy, a signal honour is about to be conferred on you. You shall drive my curricle with Miss Nell as your passenger."

"Oh, yes, that's a splendid notion!" exclaimed Catherine. "I shall easily manage on the horse for that short distance!"

"Perhaps, but I have a better scheme," said Pamyngton. "That is if you have no objection to it. I propose to tie your sister's horse to the back of the curricle, and take you up before me on Eversley's."

"Oh!" The short exclamation was almost a gasp.

"It is, after all, for a very short distance," said Pamyngton, persuasively.

There was a moment's silence, then she said, in an embarrassed tone "Yes — yes, I suppose it is. I am quite willing to try riding Nell's horse, but — but if you feel this is a better way —"

"Oh, yes, Katie, I think so," put in Eleanor. "And as it is dark no one will notice, you know."

"A capital notion I'm sure," approved Freddy, meeting Pamyngton's eye in a brief but meaning look. "Come then Miss Nell, we must get you settled."

This could only be done by the two gentlemen making a chair of their arms for Eleanor so that they could carry her to the curricle, where there was a slight difficulty in placing her comfortably aboard.

"I've always wanted to try my hand with your bays," remarked Freddy to Pamyngton, as he mounted into the vehicle. "Odd how things turn out sometimes, ain't it?"

The curricle moved slowly off, and Pamyngton lifted Catherine lightly to the saddle of the horse which they were to share. Then he mounted behind her, and sent the animal ambling gently in the wake of the vehicle.

Night was closing in, although the sky still held its summer lightness; trees and hedges were dark shadows lining the road which stretched palely ahead. At first Catherine sat stiffly within the enclosure of Pamyngton's arms, her fingers twisted in the horse's mane, staring after the curricle. She was thinking that circumstances had brought her very close in every way to this man tonight; and presently he made a remark which showed that this thought had also crossed his mind.

"We've shared quite a few adventures this evening, Katie, have we not?"

She agreed, turning her face towards him.

"Dare I hope," he continued, "that you think a little better of me now than you did at first? Perhaps it is only wishful thinking, but I fancy there is some slight leniency in your attitude towards me."

"What nonsense you do talk, sir!"

"Remember you promised to call me Pam — or at the very least, Pamyngton. And I am not talking nonsense now, I assure you. It is a matter of great importance to me that you should think well of me."

"Oh, in that case I do!" she replied, trying to speak lightly. "I am no good at all at being hard-hearted, you must know, and invariably end by forgiving everybody."

He sighed. "I often think, Katie, that whoever invented the bonnet as female headgear did a great disservice to the male section of the population."

"But why, sir — Pam?" she asked, in surprise.

"Because it so effectively conceals a female's face, and especially in this light — or should I say, dark? And since I cannot see your face, I have no notion whether or not you really mean what you say."

Impulsively, she pushed her bonnet on to the back of her head, where it hung by the strings tied under her chin.

"There! Is that better?" she asked, with her usual saucy smile.

He looked down at her and caught his breath. Her eyes were dark and lustrous in the fading light, and a night breeze blew a lock of hair across the soft curve of her cheek. He had a sudden impulse to close his arms about her, an impulse which he found surprisingly difficult to control.

When he could trust himself to speak, he said lightly, "Indeed it is. Shall we initiate a campaign to suppress all bonnets?"

"But what would the milliners do then?" she asked, with a somewhat shaky laugh.

He answered her with some nonsense which made her laugh again; and they continued talking in the same vein until they all reached the inn where a carriage was to be hired.

But Catherine had not been insensible of the atmosphere between them; and had Pamyngton given way to his impulse, he might have found her more receptive than he could ever have hoped.

Chapter XIV: A Musical Evening at the Pavilion

Like all the rooms in the Prince's summer palace, the dining-room was unbearably hot. The table, polished to perfection and laid with fine silver and glass which glistened in the light of the massive chandeliers, was abundantly spread with good food. In the place of honour sat His Royal Highness. The conventional evening dress of tight coat, white knee breeches and stockings had the unfortunate effect of accentuating his plumpness, but he radiated good humour, even if his face was somewhat flushed from wine and the heat of the room. Next to him sat Mrs. Fitzherbert, wearing a soft blue gown which admirably set off her fair colouring and golden hair, and exposed glimpses of an ample white bosom. Richard Sheridan, who was also one of the small select party, appeared to be in one of his devil-may-care moods, for he cracked frequent jokes and once went so far as to dig my Lady Berkeley in the ribs. George Brummell, immaculately dressed as usual, allowed an expression of incredulous disdain to cross his face at this departure from the conventional.

Viscount Pamyngton, who was sitting next to the Beau, noticed this and smiled. Beau Brummell, he reflected, was certainly the greatest stickler for good form of any of those present. This might have seemed extraordinary in view of the Beau's obscure connections and background; but the fact was that he had established himself as an arbiter of fashion and a valued member of the Prince's intimate circle. It was said that Prinney rarely ventured to buy a new coat without his fashionable friend's advice and approval.

Pamyngton gratefully accepted an iced dessert, and wished fervently that fans had not gone out of fashion for men. He turned to his neighbour, who, after silently surveying the dish with his eyeglass, had disdainfully waved it away.

"I'm hoping this will cool me a trifle. It's devilish hot in here. Is it always as bad as this?"

Brummel nodded. "Of course, my dear Pamyngton. Anything less than a tropical atmosphere does not suit our Prinney's taste. I collect this is your first visit to the Pavilion?"

"It is indeed. I've been at Carlton House once or twice, though, and must admit that the atmosphere was just as stifling there. But that was some years ago, and I had hoped, perhaps, that in view of the Prince's increasing — shall we say girth? — he might nowadays have favoured a slightly cooler climate."

"On the contrary. He persists in doing everything which is least conducive to good health — in eating too much, drinking too deep, and surrounding himself with intolerable heat and noise."

"The music *is* rather loud," admitted Pamyngton. "A trifle less enthusiasm, possibly, on the part of the wind instrumentalists might be no bad thing."

"My dear chap, it would be no irretrievable loss if they were all to drop dead," drawled Brummell. "Conversation is almost impossible."

"There seems to be plenty of it going on, all the same. But perhaps no one really hears what his neighbour is saying. I suppose that might not be without its advantages, at times."

"Indeed not, especially if one happens to be sitting next to Prinney when he has dined well. I believe he has embarked now on one of his interminable stories to Lady Berkeley. You must listen, Pamyngton. You'll have no difficulty in hearing him, for he means the whole table to do so. I can promise you plenty of entertainment."

Pamyngton smiled, and obediently directed his attention to the Prince, who was leaning across the table, wine glass to hand, addressing the company at large through the medium of Lady Berkeley.

"I was out one day, ma'am, with my harriers. We found a hare, but the scent was catching and uncertain, so that we could go no continuous pace at all. There was a butcher out, God damme, ma'am, and he rode slap over my favourite bitch, Ruby. I could stand it no longer, but jumping off my horse I said 'Get down, you damned rascal, or pull off your coat. None shall interfere with us, but you or I shall go back to Brighton more dead than alive.' God damme, ma'am, I threw off my coat, and the big ruffian, nothing loth, did the same by his. We fought for one hour and twenty minutes; my hunting field formed a ring round us, no one interfering, and at the end of it that big bully butcher of Brighton was carried away senseless, while I had scarcely a scratch!" His Royal Highness paused at the end of this recital, drew a deep breath and turned to Sir John Lade. "Ain't that so, Jack?"

Sir John hastened to corroborate the Prince's story, and murmurs of approbation were heard round the table. Not from Mrs. Fitzherbert, however, who frowned at the Prince and shook her head. She did not care to see him expose himself to ridicule.

Shortly afterwards, the meal came to an end and the ladies retired to the drawing-room, a circular apartment with windows looking out on to the lawn of the Pavilion. Here they chatted until ten o'clock, when the Prince led the gentlemen in, and a fresh batch of guests arrived to swell the party.

Pamyngton knew that among these would be Colonel Hailsham and his relatives. He found himself watching for them with growing impatience. They were among the last to come, and he noticed at once that Eleanor was missing. Evidently she was not sufficiently recovered from her mishap of yesterday. The Prince gave a gracious welcome to the family, more especially to Louisa and Catherine, for he had always a quick eye for an attractive female.

It was some time before Pamyngton could make his way to them. When he did, his first concern was to ask after Eleanor. He was told that she had hurt her ankle rather more than she had been willing to admit, and would be obliged to rest it for some days.

"Still, it is entirely her own fault," said Frances, "as she readily admitted afterwards. The trouble is, she's so hare-brained, she is always falling into stupid scrapes. And she's not the only one," she added, darkly, twinkling at Catherine. "I have my hands full with them, I may tell you."

"If I may say so, ma'am, there must be many who would willingly relieve you of the charge," said Pamyngton, with a gallant bow towards Louisa and Catherine.

"I don't doubt you're right," put in the Colonel, pinching Catherine's cheek, "and we mean to push them both off with some young sprig or other before long, don't we, my love, eh?"

No one answered this, as they were joined at that moment by several other new arrivals. Among these were Stephen Fullerton and his sisters, and the two officers who had been with them on the expedition yesterday, together with their wives. All enquired solicitously after Eleanor, Sally and Jane Fullerton asking permission of Frances to visit her on the following day.

In spite of the crowd now surrounding them, Pamyngton contrived to remain close to Catherine. He noticed that she was looking about the room as though in search of someone.

"I wish I knew who it was you were looking for so eagerly," he said, in a bantering tone that could only reach her ear. "I would seek him out and suggest a meeting at dawn — but certainly not with yourself."

He expected to be rewarded with one of her saucy looks and an answering quip; but to his surprise she barely glanced at him before resuming her scrutiny of the room.

After a moment, she replied, in a matter-of-fact tone, "I thought duelling was not allowed in Brighton."

He was a little disconcerted by her manner, which was cool to the point of indifference, and anxiously racked his mind for anything which he might have done to offend her afresh. After last night, he had hoped... He turned his thoughts from last night, and strove to answer her in a calm, unconcerned manner to match her own.

"I would not go so far as to say that, though it certainly isn't encouraged. Townsend has once or twice put a stop to it, so I hear."

"Townsend?" she queried, without sparing him so much as a glance.

"The Bow Street Runner who guards the Prince. You must have seen him — he's never far from the Royal side. He's here tonight."

"Oh, yes," she said, indifferently. "I had forgotten his name, that's all."

He was silent for a moment, subdued by her evident reluctance to continue the conversation.

"Are you by any chance looking for Crendon?" he asked at last, trying in desperation to rouse her to some show of interest. "If so, I may as well tell you that he won't be putting in an appearance here."

"Why not?"

That had fetched her head round for a moment, even if she did favour him with nothing but a hostile look.

"Because he is not invited." He tried to keep the satisfaction out of his voice.

She shrugged. "Oh. It's no matter — I shall be seeing him tomorrow, in any case."

Then she turned towards Stephen Fullerton, who had been watching for some time for a chance to speak to her, and proceeded to give him the benefit of a flow of bright conversation and sparkling looks.

Pamyngton reflected that women were the devil: there was no making any sense of them. He turned his attention to Louisa, who as usual seemed slightly out of the general conversation, although several people had exchanged a few remarks with her.

Presently there was a move to the Music room. The Prince was very fond of music, and on these occasions he usually called on those of his guests who were capable of it to play or sing an air to entertain the rest.

Fullerton offered his arm to Catherine to lead her into the other room. Observing this, Pamyngton followed with Louisa; but the two couples were soon separated by others entering the room, and eventually found seats a little way apart.

The Prince was prevailed upon to open the concert by singing a glee. He had a good bass voice; he performed with verve, and certainly deserved some of the generous applause which followed his performance. After that, a self-confident young lady, with bright yellow locks, played a showy pianoforte solo. The Prince begged her to favour the company with more, and even went so far as to offer to turn over the music for her; but Mrs. Fitzherbert with great presence of mind insisted that the lady looked fatigued, and must on no account be persuaded to do more than she ought, an equivocal remark which at once took the fair performer back to her chair against the wall.

Her place was taken by Frances, who had often performed before at these musical parties at the Pavilion, and knew just what would please. She played a selection of soft country airs, occasionally singing one in a melodious, though not very strong, voice.

"Your sister performs delightfully," remarked Pamyngton to Louisa, in one of the short intervals between one song and the next.

She nodded; and, looking down at her, he surprised a look of gentle melancholy on her face. No doubt the tunes Frances was playing were old family favourites, he thought, and might hold memories of happier times for the girl at his side. It was possible that she and her lover might have sung them together in the days before they had been forced to part. He watched her sympathetically while Frances struck the opening chords of her final song.

"*What's this dull town to me?*
Robin's not here…"

The plaintive tune was matched by the words. Pamyngton saw Louisa's hands clench in her lap, saw the blue eyes fill with tears. She bowed her head as a choking sob escaped her, too low for anyone but himself to hear.

Instinctively, he put out his hand and covered hers with a strong, comforting clasp.

At the same moment, Catherine glanced towards them and observed the gesture. She raised her chin a trifle, and stared defiantly away. It was quite evident that Viscount Pamyngton was the most abominable flirt. Only yesterday evening he had held her, Catherine, in his arms — even if only inadvertently — and allowed her to think…

Her thoughts broke off at this point, refusing to dwell on what she had been encouraged to believe.

When Frances rose from the pianoforte, there were some more glees, and then it was time for supper. Catherine watched Pamyngton draw Louisa's arm through his and lead her away to the supper room. She herself, in a fresh burst of lively spirits, followed with Stephen Fullerton.

There was quite a crush in the room, and at one point she found herself standing behind Mrs. Mostyn and Mrs. Drummond, although the ladies were too earnestly engaged in talking to each other to notice her. Fragments of their conversation drifted back to Catherine, one part in particular riveting her attention.

"My dear," said Mrs. Mostyn, with relish, "did you notice Pamyngton holding Louisa Denham's hand just now?"

Catherine did not catch the reply, but Mrs. Mostyn hardly waited for it before launching into further speech.

"I wasn't certain myself, yesterday, which of those two he had fixed his fancy upon. It seemed to be first one and then the other, don't you agree? In fact, I began to wonder if he meant anything at all by it. But now it does look, don't you think, Margaret, as if the elder girl will get the handkerchief?"

Catherine darted anxious looks at the people surrounding her but soon realized that probably no one else could have heard the remarks. They were all too busy chattering away themselves while her escort had concerned himself with finding her a chair. Presently he steered her towards it; and the remainder of the evening passed without her having any very clear idea of what was happening around her.

Chapter XV: Plans for an Assignation

When Catherine came downstairs the next morning, it was in the hope that Captain Crendon would soon present himself on their doorstep so that she could discuss with him the plans she had made for keeping her assignation with Oliver that evening.

They did have some morning callers. Sally and Jane Fullerton came to see Eleanor, who was sitting with her foot supported on a stool and wearing a very glum countenance until her friends put in an appearance, when she cheered up at once. But as the morning wore on and there was still no sign of Crendon, Catherine decided that she must go out in search of him. She eventually managed to persuade Louisa to accompany her to Donaldson's, ostensibly to change a book. She buoyed herself up with the hope that she was almost certain to come across the Captain somewhere on the Steyne, as on a fine day practically everyone in Brighton could be found there.

What she did not bargain for was meeting Pamyngton, yet he was almost the first person they encountered whom they knew. He was on horseback in company with several others, among them Frederick Eversley. Although both gentlemen bowed to the young ladies, it was evident that they could not conveniently stop at that moment, however much they might have wished it. Pamyngton, indeed, glanced back more than once.

"How well he sits a horse!" exclaimed Louisa, suddenly.

"Who do you mean? Mr. Eversley?" Catherine was deliberately obtuse.

"Oh, yes, I suppose so, but it was not Mr. Eversley I was speaking of. But then he does everything well — Lord Pamyngton, I mean — and he is so kind, so understanding."

Catherine ostentatiously stifled a yawn. "Oh, yes, so you've said before. My dear Lou, you must be careful, or you will become a dead bore on that subject."

"I wish I could make you see how good he is," said Louisa, wistfully.

"Why? One of us going into raptures over him is enough at a time," replied her sister, with a scornful laugh.

Louisa was a little hurt by this reply, and said no more for a while. They reached Donaldson's and were about to pass inside when, to her relief, Catherine saw Captain Crendon sitting alone on one of the benches in front of the building. It crossed her mind that he wore a somewhat dejected air, but she was too intent on her plans to concentrate on this thought. She hastily touched Louisa's arm.

"There is Captain Crendon," she said, quickly. "I must see him for a moment alone, so do you go in, Lou, and I'll join you presently."

Louisa hesitated. "I ought not to leave you alone with him. Fanny wouldn't like it."

"What, in full stare of everyone passing by? Don't be absurd, Lou! One can be too missish."

"Oh, very well," replied her sister, reluctantly. "But I do wish, Katie, you didn't show such an interest in that young man. Everyone says he is not quite — oh all right! I am going."

She went into the library, and Catherine approached Crendon. He came slowly to his feet on seeing her, but did not look overjoyed.

"I've been waiting in all morning hoping you would call," she began, impetuously. "Why did you not come?"

"Naturally I'm flattered," he drawled. "All the same, I can't quite imagine —"

"Stupid!" she exclaimed, impatiently. "Can you have forgotten my appointment with Oliver?"

He stared at her for a moment. "With Oliver? Who the devil — oh, that! Yes, I must confess it had completely escaped my memory. I've had rather a lot on my plate, lately."

"Well, after all, you did volunteer to escort me. But if you don't find it convenient," she said, with dignity, "pray think no more about it. Good morning, Captain Crendon."

She was about to sweep on but he touched her arm to detain her.

"Not so fast — there's no need to get in your high ropes. I said nothing about convenience, only about having forgotten in the press of more urgent concerns. Of course I'll take you to Rottingdean to meet this clergyman fellow — between eight and nine o'clock this evening, wasn't it? Tell me where and when, and I'll meet you with my curricle."

As far as she was able, Catherine had already laid her plans. The family were to dine out that evening, but Eleanor would remain at home on account of her injury. Although she declared that she would be quite content to remain alone, provided she could have first turn at the latest novel from the library, Catherine had insisted on staying behind to keep her younger sister company. She had been almost foiled in this by Louisa, who had persisted in offering herself in Catherine's place until Frances settled the argument.

"No, no, let Katie immolate herself on the altar of unselfishness if she wishes!" she declared, laughing. "You are always too ready a sacrifice, Lou!"

Once this was settled, it meant that at least Catherine would be at home and relatively unsupervised that evening. How she would contrive to slip out and meet Crendon was another problem, which must be left until the event. It might even entail taking Eleanor into her confidence; though she was reluctant to do this, knowing how indiscreet her sister could be at times. For the present, she arranged to meet the Captain in a narrow side turning quite close to the house, as near to half past seven as she could manage.

"And leave your curricle somewhere not too far away in as inconspicuous a place as possible," she warned him, "for it will still be light, and we shall be perilously near the house."

He undertook to do this, and they parted.

Although Captain Crendon had forgotten the arrangement made a week previously, Pamyngton had not. Riding past Donaldson's, he noticed Catherine in conversation with Crendon, and at once was reminded of her appointment in Rottingdean for that evening. He frowned. If only the fair Katie were not such an impulsive little wretch when she was in the grip of an idea! How did she think she could trust any man to keep the line when she made secret assignations such as this with him? It was a thousand pities that she had asked Crendon to help her, instead of himself. That charm of hers — the quicksilver blend of demureness and sauciness — what man could hope to withstand it for long? And Crendon was notoriously a womaniser: more, he was known at present to be in very deep water financially.

He shrugged. That side of things did not signify, of course. The girl had relatives to protect her, and by all accounts they were quite equal to the task of fending off impecunious suitors. The question of placing her reputation in jeopardy was another matter. There were plenty of curious eyes and ears in Brighton, and malicious tongues to finish their task. What could be done to safeguard her?

He might, of course, offer himself as her escort in place of Crendon. He pondered this for a moment. No, there seemed no point in that after her cold reception of him yesterday. Why had she been so hostile, he wondered? It might have been different if he had given way to the impulse which had nearly overcome him when she had been so close to him on the expedition to Devil's Dyke. Whatever her reasons might be, it was obvious that she would spurn any offers of help from himself.

Besides, he had to admit that he was not facing the issue squarely. Her reputation was no safer in his hands than in Crendon's. Whichever of them happened to be seen in her company alone at that time of night, there would be gossip. The thing was, he did not trust Crendon. Supposing he went beyond the line of what was pleasing, and Catherine Denham were to find herself for the second time stranded on the roadside as dusk was falling? Who then would rescue her? Perhaps the gallant gentleman of her first adventure; he seemed to be somewhere in the vicinity, as they had encountered him at White Hawk Fair.

At this point in his meditations, Freddy Eversley demanded to be told why he was wearing such a damned grim expression.

"Was I?" Pamyngton passed this off with a laugh. "I dare say it's the effect of yesterday's musical evening at the Pavilion."

"Dev'lish affairs, ain't they?" agreed his younger companion. "The best bit to my mind was when Sheridan got up to his tricks with old Lady Sefton, dressing up in togs he'd borrowed from the Runner Townsend, and pretending to arrest her. For an old man, he's a lively spark."

"Did he? I missed that."

"So you might," replied Freddy, with a sly look, "for you were doing the polite to the entrancing Denham girls. Tell me, Pam, if it ain't an awkward question, which of 'em is it to be?"

"Damme, never say you're starting off on that tack," said Pamyngton in disgust. "Everyone seems to be in a conspiracy to get me married off, it seems."

"Well, high time, old fellow, now ain't it? Unless you've quite fixed to go to your grave a bachelor."

"Whatever my views on the subject," retorted Pamyngton, dryly, "it will always be the greatest comfort to me to know that my friends show such a flattering interest in my concerns."

"Like me to stick my head in a barrel, would you?" grinned his companion. "Be easy — I'll say no more."

He kept to his promise the more readily because their companions drew them into conversation at that moment.

After he had returned to The Ship, Pamyngton found himself brooding again over Catherine's proposed escapade. He wondered what arrangements she had made for meeting Crendon, and how she intended to slip away without her family knowing where she was going. Since he could not ask her directly, there seemed no way of discovering these things. It came to him forcibly that he had to be sure of her safety, no matter to what lengths he must go to achieve this end.

There seemed only one way open to him, and that was not a course to commend itself. In spite of this, though, he knew that he must keep watch over her that evening.

By mutual consent, Eleanor and Catherine had eaten their evening meal early, and were now sitting in a small parlour at the back of the house, reading. At least, Eleanor was reading, but her sister was making only a thin pretence of doing so. Every now and then she kept glancing at the clock; and as its tinkling chimes told seven, she yawned ostentatiously.

"Oh, dear, I am so tired!"

Eleanor looked up with a frown of irritation.

"Well, if you are, why don't you sit still for a bit and stop that everlasting fidgeting? You're quite ruining my concentration, and I've just reached a most absorbing episode in this book!"

"I'm sorry," replied Catherine, contritely. "Since you're enjoying your book so much, and I only seem to be disturbing you, perhaps you will not mind if I go up to bed?"

Eleanor put down the book and stared at her sister. "Go to bed? At seven o'clock? Whoever heard of such a thing?"

"Well, I really am uncommonly tired."

"Tired! You must be ill, Katie, before you'll talk of retiring at this time of day! You'd better let the children's nurse have a look at you."

"Oh, no, I don't want any fuss. It is simply that I'm tired — after all, we were very late at the Pavilion last night —"

"Stuff! We've had scores of late nights since we came here, and when we were in London for the season; yet I've never once heard you complain before of feeling tired, and wanting to go off to bed. There *must* be something wrong with you."

"Well, perhaps I do have just a little bit of a headache — nothing to speak of, really —"

"That settles it," said Eleanor, firmly. "Ring the bell and we'll ask Nurse to step downstairs for a moment. It's no use protesting — you know very well Fanny would insist on it if she were here."

Catherine was silent for a moment, while she turned over in her mind what was the best thing to do. There would be little difficulty in persuading the children's nurse that she was ill and ought to go to bed; but if she did so, she would certainly not be free of cosseting attentions for at least the next hour. Even after that, it might be difficult to escape from the house, as Nurse would be keeping a watchful eye on her. All things considered, perhaps she had better tell her sister the truth — or part of it, at any rate.

"I must say," remarked Eleanor, judicially, "you don't look to be ill. Are you going to ring that bell, or must I hobble across the floor to do it myself?"

Catherine sat up suddenly. "All right," she said, in a more alert tone. "You win. I'm perfectly well — never felt better, in fact."

"Ah, I was beginning to suspect as much! Then just what are you up to, Katie?"

"The fact is," said Catherine, slowly, "I had promised to meet Captain Crendon."

Eleanor stared again. "A secret assignation, do you mean? Oh, Katie, is that wise?"

Catherine shrugged. "I don't know — perhaps not, but what does it signify? I want to go."

"Whereto?"

"Oh, just for a drive."

"But suppose you are seen? People are sure to talk."

"We won't be. He is not calling for me at the house. We've arranged to meet in that lane just a step down the road. Hardly anyone ever uses it, and, anyway, most people are still indoors at this hour. He's to leave his carriage somewhere nearby, but in a spot that isn't overlooked. It will go splendidly never fear!"

"It is prodigiously romantic," said Eleanor, with enthusiasm. "But — you're not *eloping* with him, are you, Katie? Because I really don't think I should let you — Papa and Mama will make my life a misery if I do!"

"No, silly," replied her sister, scornfully. "It's not at all like that."

"Then what is it?" asked Eleanor, puzzled. "You don't need to take all this trouble to go out with the Captain, for Fanny has allowed you to go driving with him once already. There must be something else — something more than you have told me!"

"Well, perhaps there is," conceded Catherine. "But it's of no use to pester me about it, as I don't mean to tell you anything more at present. But I can assure you that I shall return here safe and sound by about ten o'clock."

"That's all very well, but if I am expected to cover up for you," said Eleanor, obstinately, "I think I should be allowed to know what's afoot."

"Oh, and did you think to tell me before you dashed off into that crowded fairground and had Pamyngton and myself hunting high and low for you for an age?" demanded Catherine, indignantly. "If you're determined to be a spoilsport, Nell, after all the trouble you caused that evening —"

"Oh, very well! Don't go on so! Of course I don't mean to spoil your fun. As long as you know what you're doing," she added, darkly. "They do say that the Captain is no end of a lady-killer."

"Trust me to look out for that." She rose and flung her arms around her sister. "You're a dear, Nell, and I will tell you all about it soon, I promise. I'm not doing this for myself, although you may think it's just one of my hare-brained starts. But I can say nothing more at present." She broke off and made for the door. "I'll just get my pelisse and bonnet, and then I'll be off. Fanny and the rest ought not to be home before midnight, but if they are, you'll know what to say."

Eleanor laughed. "Yes — that you went to bed early with the headache, and don't wish to be disturbed!"

Chapter XVI: The Watcher

Catherine had chosen a time of day when she judged that there would be few people about in West Street; and after slipping quietly from the house, she was able to reach the meeting place unobserved. A man loitering in the lane turned as she approached. With some relief, she recognized Crendon.

"So you managed to come," he greeted her. "I was quite prepared for a longer wait. The curricle's round the corner in a quiet enough spot, so with any luck we should get off without attracting notice." He glanced approvingly at her bonnet, the brim of which almost obscured her face. "You did well to choose one like that."

"I particularly detest this," answered Catherine, speaking in a whisper. "I can't imagine whatever possessed me to buy it at all."

"It answers the purpose admirably tonight. Come!"

He drew her arm through his and walked with her briskly down the lane and round the corner into another street. Here the curricle was waiting in the charge of a skinny youth who closed his hand tightly on the coin which Crendon thrust into it, then vanished silently down a nearby alley.

At first, they made a wide detour in order to avoid the ever-popular Steyne and the sea front, where there was a risk of meeting someone they knew. After Brighton's busier thoroughfares had been left behind, they joined the coast road once more.

The white cliffs stretched invitingly ahead, with the sea, blue-grey and deceptively smooth, at their foot. A few gulls were circling, uttering the plaintive cries of their kind. The sun was setting in a burst of red and gold. It was a balmy evening, and the scene was rich in beauty; yet Catherine could derive no pleasure from it. She was unaccountably ill at ease.

They talked little, and only of trivialities when they did find anything to say. It was evident that Crendon was as preoccupied as she was herself.

Dusk was gathering as they came into Rottingdean. Crendon pulled up, and leaned over to hand his passenger down.

"Can you manage? I see your man's already there, by the pond. He's coming over now. How long do you want?"

"Only a quarter of an hour," replied Catherine. "I daren't stay longer — perhaps not even as long as that."

Crendon nodded, and wheeled the vehicle to face in the opposite direction. At the same moment, Oliver Seaton reached Catherine's side. He touched his hat distantly to Crendon, who replied with a flourish of his whip before moving away down the road.

"I'm deuced glad to see you, Katie!" exclaimed Oliver, taking both her hands in his for a moment. "I wasn't counting on your being able to come, knowing how difficult it would be for you. And indeed," he added, "since our last meeting, I've been plagued with remorse. I ought not to have asked you to meet me clandestinely in this way and I must certainly never do so again."

"Oh, fiddle!" replied Catherine, inelegantly. "I didn't come here to listen to your moralizing. Do you or don't you want to hear some news of Louisa?"

"There is no other subject that matters, God help me. I have tried earnestly to keep my thoughts away from her, but to no purpose."

It was spoken with a controlled despair that frayed the girl's already overwrought sensibilities. Her lips twisted.

"I'm bound to tell you that she seems to be making more success of keeping her thoughts away from you. She is always praising Pamyngton of late," she replied, almost brutally. "He's become quite a favourite with her."

He said nothing for a few moments, staring at the ground. "And Pamyngton?" he asked, looking up at last.

She gave an unhappy shrug. "Oh, who can tell? He is certainly most attentive, even to the point of holding her hand at a musical evening at the Pavilion. But this does not prelude his using words to others which —" she choked a little — "which could easily give them the impression that they were the true object of his attentions. But I suppose it serves them right if they're so foolish as to take him seriously," she finished, with a defiant toss of her head which was belied somewhat by a slight unsteadiness of the lips.

"By —!"

Oliver controlled the oath by a great effort; his brow was like a thundercloud. Catherine shrank away from him, recognizing the rare anger of her childhood playmate. He took a few moments to master his feelings, and when he did speak, it was in a dangerously controlled tone.

"What you tell me convinces me that this man is unworthy of the fairest, gentlest creature —" His voice trembled momentarily, and he paused to steady it. "Leave this to me, Katie. In such a case, I feel justified in breaking my promise to your parents."

"You mean to see Lou?" demanded Catherine. "Do you want me to tell her you are here and —"

He shook his head. "No. Keep silent for the present. I must think over what is best to do. I do not think it likely that I shall ask you to meet me here again; but should I decide that it's really necessary, I will contrive to send you a message somehow or other." He looked up as he heard the carriage returning. "Here comes your escort. Good-bye, Catherine, and forgive me if you can for entangling you in my concerns. You're a good child."

A good child! After she had climbed aboard the vehicle and they were homeward bound once more, she brooded ruefully on this remark. She would have done better to have held her tongue about Louisa and Pamyngton, and pretended that all was right. But the pent-up resentment of the past twenty-four hours had been bound to find some outlet.

She was sorry now that she had given Oliver the benefit of it; she had not intended that. She wondered what he would do, and hoped fervently that she had not precipitated any action on his part that could only add to his present distress.

"You are not particularly lively company this evening, Miss Catherine," Crendon remarked, after a while.

"I suppose not. I'm sorry — I was thinking."

"And who is the fortunate subject of your thoughts?"

"Since you ask, Oliver is."

"Oliver!" he repeated, mockingly. "I see how it is — you are falling in love with the fellow yourself."

"I am not so addicted to falling in love," she retorted, with dignity, "as you seem to imagine!"

"That is a pity." He regarded her mockingly. "I had hoped that you made quite a habit of it, and might presently make your way round to me."

She was a little taken aback. If the remark had been made in a crowded room on some social occasion, it would have been easy to treat it as just another light-hearted gallantry. But here, miles from home in the fast gathering shadows and alone with a man with whom she had been acquainted for so short a time, she felt vaguely uneasy.

"I am not in the mood for flirtatious remarks," she said, coldly.

"Who said anything about flirting?"

He turned towards her, his eyes fixed on her in that intense look which she remembered from the last time they had travelled along this road together. As on that occasion, her pulses gave a sudden leap; but this time, it was as much from fear as excitement.

It was with a sense of relief that she heard the pounding of hoofs on the road behind them. Evidently they were not the only travellers abroad that evening on this particular stretch of the highway.

"There's someone behind us," she said, glad of the chance to change the subject.

He withdrew his eyes from her, and glanced briefly to the rear.

"A solitary horseman," he replied, indifferently. "I'll slow up so that he can pass."

He drew the curricle in to a walking pace. The horseman showed no inclination to pass, however. Instead, he slowed his pace to maintain the same distance as before from the vehicle.

"Damn the fellow!" exclaimed Crendon, in disgust. "He was galloping a moment since, and there's plenty of room for him to get by. Perhaps he doesn't trust the light. Oh, well, no point in hanging about — let's shake him off."

He urged his horses forward to a spanking trot.

"Oh, pray don't let us go too fast!" pleaded Catherine. "Recollect what happened last time!"

He laughed. "No fear of that on this road! But you'd best hold tight, all the same."

He held the pace for another five minutes or so, then slowed. The hoof beats still sounded behind them; and looking back, Catherine and he could faintly discern the outline of a horse and rider at no great distance away.

"Hell and the devil!" said Crendon. "You'd think the fellow was deliberately dogging our trail!"

"Pay no heed to him," pleaded Catherine, alarmed lest Crendon should respond to the seeming challenge, by setting a headlong pace that would only land them in trouble a second time. "What does it matter whether he is behind us or in front?"

"Not a whit, I suppose," he answered, with a shrug.

The incident seemed to have put him slightly out of humour, and to Catherine's relief he showed no inclination to return to the conversation at the point where they had left it. Neither of them spoke at all for several miles until they were coming in to the outskirts of Brighton. By this time it was dark; they could no longer see the unknown rider in the distance, but they could still hear the faint clopping of hoofs.

"Damned fellow!" grunted Crendon. Then, dismissing the subject as unprofitable — "When are you to meet your clergyman friend again?"

Catherine started out of her reverie. "He said not at all — or, at least, only if some emergency occurred. In that case, he is to get a message to me by some means or other — but I don't think it will arise."

"Well, I am at your service if you should require me," he said.

She thanked him, but it was in a constrained manner very different from the previous time. Either he noticed this or else he was wrapped up in some thoughts of his own, for their conversation languished, finally dying out altogether as by devious ways they reached North Street. Here Catherine suggested that she should be set down at the junction with

West Street. Crendon did not oppose her in the slightest, but parted from her with scant ceremony and not a single backward glance.

She was starting to walk briskly down West Street when she heard a horseman behind her, moving at a very slow pace. At once she thought of the solitary traveller who had been in the rear of the curricle on the journey from Rottingdean. She turned her head quickly to catch a glimpse of him. He passed beneath a street light and she recognized him with a sharp intake of breath.

It was Pamyngton.

Anger flared up in her. She stopped still, waiting until he came up to her.

"You!" she said, in tones of contempt. "It was you behind us on the road — don't attempt to deny it!"

He dismounted, and crooked a finger at a lad who came forward out of the shadows.

"Take my animal to The Ship, Jack," he directed.

The boy touched his cap, moving off smartly with the horse. Pamyngton turned to Catherine, who still stood accusingly before him.

"I have no intention of denying it," he said quietly.

"I suppose you will say that there's no reason why you should not be on the King's Highway as well as anyone else!"

"I could do so, of course, with some justification. However, I don't propose to offer such an insult to your intelligence, so be easy on that score."

"Then you admit that you were spying on me?" she exclaimed indignantly.

"Do you think we might walk on?" he asked in a soothing tone. "There is something a little out of the ordinary in a lady and gentleman having a heated conversation in a poorly lit street, don't you agree? It might be remarked by curious passers-by. If you will allow me to give you my arm to your brother-in-law's house —"

"Never! After what you have done tonight, I don't wish to see you or speak to you again!"

"Dramatic, but scarcely practicable," he replied, calmly, "We are likely to be thrown in company fairly frequently as long as both of us remain in Brighton."

"Then I shall leave the place tomorrow!"

"And run away from me a second time?" A note of amusement crept into his voice. "I hope your plans will have better fortune on this occasion. Or would you care to furnish me with details of them, so that I can come to your aid should anything go wrong?"

"You are insufferable!" she exclaimed angrily, turning on her heel and starting to walk quickly away.

He had no difficulty in keeping up with her.

"Yes, I realize that I must be, as you would scarce acknowledge me when we met this morning. Though what I had done to deserve your censure then, is more than I can imagine."

Womanlike, Catherine seized on this tacit admission of present guilt. "So you do admit that I have just cause to be vexed with you now?"

"I freely admit everything, in the hope that making a clean breast of things may earn me some mitigation of sentence."

"Everything is a joke to you — you refuse to treat anything or anyone seriously!" she declared in exasperation.

"You are mistaken, Katie." His tone altered subtly. "I take anything to do with you very seriously indeed. That is why — after many misgivings — I decided to follow you and Crendon this evening."

"That's all very well!" she retorted. "I dare say you make exactly the same remark to other females, too — to Louisa, for instance."

"Your sister?" A note of puzzlement entered his voice.

"Yes, my sister. Don't think everyone hasn't noticed the way you hang about her. Why, even I heard it gossiped of, the other evening at the Pavilion!"

"The devil you did!"

"Oh, well," she said, sarcastically, "you must expect all your attentions to females to be the subject of gossip, an eligible bachelor like yourself!"

"I have the strongest urge at the moment," he said, taking her arm and bringing her to a halt, "to — do you know what?"

Her eyes flickered for a moment towards his face, then quickly dropped away.

"I neither know, nor care, sir," she returned coldly.

"I have a strong urge to spank you," he finished. "And devil take it, I think it might be the best way of handling you!"

She shook off his arm and drew herself up to her full height; which unfortunately for the effect, only succeeded in bringing her on a level with his shoulders.

"Leave me, Lord Pamyngton," she commanded. "As I said before, I don't wish to set eyes on you again!"

"As you wish."

He bowed, and watched her finish the short distance to the Hailshams' house. Once she was safely there, he turned away.

Chapter XVII: A Summons

It was after three o'clock in the morning, but Raggett's Club was crowded and play was in full swing. Colonel Hailsham, who had dropped in on his way home from a private card party in order to have an urgent word with a fellow officer whom he knew to be in the club, paused at one of the tables to watch for a moment. He frowned.

Four men were seated round the table, three of them in various stages of dishabille. Two had discarded their coats; one of them was leaning his left arm on the table, the fine lawn sleeve of his shirt rapidly soaking up a splash of wine which had been spilt from a bottle. The third man had untied his cravat, and the points of his collar were wilting. Only the remaining member of the group looked as trim as when he had first sat down to play, all those hours ago; his dark, slightly sardonic face gave no hint to the onlooker that he had been losing steadily all night.

All the same, John Hailsham knew it; and his frown deepened as he took his way out of the club and so home to bed.

It was not long afterwards that the group at the table finished play. One of the men yawned and reached for his coat.

"Well, I'm for bed, gentlemen," he said, in slightly slurred accents. "How d'ye make the reckoning, Fawley?"

The man addressed made a few rapid calculations and named the sums involved. There was a rustle of paper and chink of coin as three of the men paid their debts. The fourth pushed his chair back and rose slowly from the table.

"I haven't the sum about me at present." He spoke coolly enough though an onlooker in a more sober state than his companions might have noticed a set look around his mouth. "I.O.U.s will answer, I imagine, for the moment?"

"Oh, ay — need you ask, my dear Crendon?" replied Fawley readily and the other two nodded their agreement.

There was a writing desk against the wall a little way off. Crendon crossed to it, drew pen and paper towards him, and presently returned to hand over to his companions acknowledgements of debts to the value of almost a thousand pounds.

"At my earliest, gentlemen." He bowed. "Perhaps a day or two — I have urgent business which takes me up to Town —"

"You going along with Hailsham and Bickerstaff, then?" asked Fawley, as he stowed the note carelessly in his pocket, and began tying his cravat. "Heard they were off up to London for a spell — not another invasion scare, is it, d'ye think? Makes you wonder when the military start movin' about, don't it?"

"My lips, of course, are sealed," returned Crendon with a strained smile.

He made some excuse not to leave at the same time as his companions and later strolled home alone along the sea front. There was little light from the clouded moon; the sea was a black, heaving mass beneath the paler dark of the sky. He gazed out over it, leaning on a railing and hearing as in a dream the rhythmic slapping of waves on the beach and the hiss of pebbles caught in the undertow. His future seemed as dark as the scene before him. He had sold what he could, borrowed where he could to meet his enormous gaming debts; now he had come to the end of his resources.

After a while he walked on, leaving the sea front and taking his way to his lodging off St. James's Street. He let himself in, for his servants had been told to go to bed, and, throwing himself down in a chair, brooded for a while. Presently he roused, stood up and poured a drink from one of the bottles standing on the sideboard. He tossed the liquor off, slammed down the glass, and crossed the room to enter another parlour. He paused on the threshold, seeing no light within. Cursing under his breath, he seized a branched candlestick from the first room and carried it through to the second, setting it down on a large roll-top bureau. He flung back the lid of this, releasing a small avalanche of papers.

He seized a handful, gave them a cursory glance, then flung them on the floor, setting his heel upon them.

"Damned bills, blister it! Nothing but damned bills! Hell and the devil! What's to be done?"

He leaned over the untidy heap of paper extracting a long leather case from underneath it. He opened this, and stood gazing thoughtfully for some time at a handsome silver-mounted pistol.

Suddenly he snapped the case shut, and laughed harshly.

"No, b'God!" he said, aloud. "There might be some who'd seek that way out, but not for me. I think I know a trick worth six of that."

He set the case down, swept the pile of bills aside until he had cleared a space at the bureau, then seated himself before it. After some difficulty, he succeeded in finding pen, ink and paper. He wrote the heading, then paused chewing the end of his pen thoughtfully for several moments.

At length inspiration came, and he wrote steadily while outside his window the sky lightened, turned pearl-grey, became streaked with the first pale tints of dawn.

"Captain Crendon has called, madam."

Frances started, glanced hastily round at her sisters, who had only just finished a late breakfast, and shook her head.

"Deny us, Waddon. It is too early in the day — say the Colonel is absent from home, and the ladies are not yet ready to receive visitors."

"Very good, Madam."

The butler was about to withdraw, but Catherine cried out impatiently. "Nonsense, Fanny! We are all properly dressed, and although it may be a little early for morning calls, what else is there to do, pray?"

Frances glanced at her, then at the butler. "Yes, but — I think —" She broke off and shrugged. "Oh, very well, since you wish it! Show the Captain in, Waddon."

The door closed behind the manservant.

"I must tell you, Katie," Frances said quickly, in a lowered tone, "that John desired me last night to warn you girls off Crendon. It seems he's getting himself up to his ears in debt — indeed John says his case is desperate; so it's of no use at all to give him any encouragement. If he's come to take you for a drive, you must make some excuse. Hush! Here he comes."

Captain Crendon was admitted, and from the first moment appeared unusually affable. He had evidently come to please. He enquired after Eleanor's injury, which was now quite recovered; commiserated with Frances on the temporary loss of her husband, who had a few hours ago posted to London with Colonel Bickerstaff; and praised Louisa's embroidery. Half an hour or more passed very pleasantly away before he rose to take his leave.

As he did so, he requested Catherine for the pleasure of her company on a short drive that afternoon.

She hesitated, looking at Frances, who quickly took the cue.

"You have an appointment with the dressmaker for this afternoon, I think, Katie?"

"Oh, yes, of course," answered Catherine quickly. "I'm sorry Captain Crendon."

"Perhaps tomorrow then? I am at your disposal either morning or afternoon."

"I fear the next few days are so occupied with engagements of one kind or another that we shall scarcely have time to draw breath," said Frances, with a laugh.

"Yes, that is so indeed, we've been obliged to refuse several invitations," added Catherine, giving him a regretful look. "I am sorry, sir."

He was no fool, and saw very well how it was; but he gave no sign, taking his leave with calm assurance.

"Well, I never thought you'd pay any heed to what Fanny said!" exclaimed Eleanor in surprise, after he had gone. "You could have knocked me down with a feather! I quite thought he was a prodigious favourite with you!"

"Perhaps I did find him interesting to begin with," admitted Catherine. "He's an unusual person. He doesn't set out to flatter a female as most gentlemen do — in fact, at times he can be almost rude! It's quite intriguing at first, for sometimes one gets a little bored by endless gallantries; but once the novelty has worn off —" She shrugged.

"It's worn off uncommon quickly, I'd say," retorted Eleanor. "Why, only the other evening, you were still interested enough in him to —"

She was stopped in mid-sentence by an unusually fierce glare from her sister.

"What's this?" demanded Frances instantly on the alert.

"Oh, nothing," said Catherine, hurriedly. "You know how Nell rattles on. Anyway, we promised the Fullertons that we'd go there this morning if you recollect. I'm going upstairs to get ready."

"Eleanor!" said Frances, sternly, when Catherine had shut the door behind her. "What is all this?"

"Oh, only girlish confidences, Fan," returned her younger sister, airily. "Be easy."

"I think perhaps," put in Louisa, with some idea of providing a distraction, "we ought to follow Katie's example, and get ready for our outing."

Meanwhile, Catherine had been halted on her way upstairs by one of the footmen, who handed her a letter.

"The gentleman who's just left desired me to give this to you, ma'am."

She took it, opening her eyes wide; then turned away and hurried for the shelter of her bedroom.

Here she locked the door, and, moving over to the window, opened the letter.

Consumed with curiosity, she was so eager to read it as quickly as possible that she was scarcely able to take in the sense at first. She read it a second time more slowly.

It was written in the terse style she would have expected from Crendon. He wrote that he had chanced across Oliver Seaton, and that Oliver urgently wanted to see her again. He was now removed from Rottingdean and staying at Pyecombe, where he could meet her at any time of day she cared to arrange.

"I shall call on you this morning and try to get Mrs. Hailsham's permission to take you driving again," wrote Crendon. "If this ruse fails, you must think of something else, then let me know a time and place to take you up. A message to my lodging; or I shall be hanging about outside Donaldson's most of the morning should you be able to see me briefly there. But speed is essential — come today if at all possible, tomorrow at the latest."

She stood gazing out of the window, deep in thought. Oliver had said it was unlikely that he would need to see her again. What could have happened to make him change his mind, moreover to make the matter one of such urgency? A vivid imagination would usually supply her readily with several answers to any speculation, but this time she could think of nothing. All the more reason, then, to go to Oliver at once and find out for certain. How was this to be achieved? More thought was needed on this point.

She was still brooding when she heard the door knob rattle, and Louisa's voice calling to her.

"Katie? Are you there? I can't get in."

She started, pushed the letter hastily down the front of her dress and flew to unlock the door. Louisa stood outside, looking puzzled.

"Why did you lock yourself in? You don't usually do so."

"Oh, I — I think I must have done it in absence of mind. I didn't realize I had," stammered Catherine.

Louisa gave her a thoughtful look. "I came to see if you would do up the top buttons on my dress. The maid's with Nell, and it seemed a pity to disturb her for that."

"Yes, of course. Come over by the window."

"Katie," went on Louisa, while her sister was performing this small service for her, "I don't wish to pry but — are you in love with the Captain?"

"Captain Crendon? Of course not! Why should you think so?"

"Well, I did just wonder. You've seemed very taken with him on the occasions when he's been in company with us. And then there was what Nell said —"

"Oh, Nell!" exclaimed Catherine, impatiently. "You know how she makes a to-do over nothing!"

"Yes, perhaps. But I know she's very indiscreet, too, and it did seem to me that she was about to disclose something which you'd rather Fanny didn't hear — something to do with you and Captain Crendon."

Catherine finished the last button and turned Louisa towards her.

"If you want to know, she was. But it's not what you think — or what she thinks, either, come to that. I can't tell you now, Lou, but I think I may be able to do so soon; and then you'll see that it's more to do with you than with anyone. No, it's of no use asking me, for I can't and won't say more at present. But one thing you can be certain of — I'm not in love with Captain Crendon, nor ever likely to be!"

Understandably, this view was not shared by the footman who had handed her Crendon's letter, and who was presently despatched secretly to the Captain's lodging with an answer.

Chapter XVIII: A Closed Carriage

The call on the Fullertons, originally planned to last an hour or two, was extended to include eating nuncheon with them and staying on as long into the afternoon as Frances Hailsham and her sisters could manage. This suited both Frances and Eleanor, as they had no pressing engagements for that day; but Louisa and Catherine were obliged to leave at half-past two as they both had an appointment with the dressmaker, whose premises were situated in one of the lanes off North Street.

Louisa's spirits had lately shown so much improvement that Frances had judged it a good moment to try the tonic effect of a new gown on her sister. Catherine was already having one made, and was due for a fitting; so Louisa was to accompany her and look over the lengths of material in the shop to see if anything there took her fancy.

When they arrived, the dressmaker at once whisked Catherine away into an inner room, and Louisa was left to wander around the shop on her own. She soon became absorbed in examining the rolls of muslin, gauze and silk which the assistant was only too pleased to show her, and did not notice the passing of time.

She was just trying to decide between a very pretty pale blue muslin embroidered with tiny white flowers and a plain lilac one, when the dressmaker reappeared.

"Is my sister finished?" asked Louisa. "I would like her opinion on which of these materials to choose."

"Oh, yes, ma'am, but I'm afraid she didn't wait. She asked me to tell you that she has a call to make somewhere else, but you are not to trouble to keep the carriage waiting for her, as she will take another conveyance home later on."

Louisa let the muslin slip from her fingers back on to the counter, and stared at the woman.

"A call somewhere else?" she repeated. "How odd — I knew nothing of it. But why did she not tell me herself? She must have walked through the shop while I was busy looking through these materials. Surely, she wouldn't have gone straight past me without saying anything?"

"No, she didn't come through the shop, ma'am. She said she was in a hurry, so I let her out through the door to the house."

The dressmaker looked doubtfully at Louisa, as though she sensed something wrong. Observing this, Louisa decided to say no more. Whatever impulse had made Catherine act in this way, there was no point in starting any gossip. A good many Brighton ladies patronized this woman, and no doubt her tongue would wag readily while she was attending to them.

"Very well," she said, drawing on her gloves. "Thank you for delivering the message. I think I will come in another time to decide which of these delightful materials to choose for my new gown."

The dressmaker escorted her to the door, where the Hailshams' carriage was already waiting to take her home. As Louisa stepped inside, she ordered the coachman to drive round into the lane on the other side of the building, where her sister would have come out. Arrived there, she lowered the window and thrust her head out to peer intently up and down the short street, but there was no sign of Catherine.

She sighed. Where in the world could the tiresome girl have gone? On their way here, she made no mention of any other call she wished to pay; she must have been seized by one of her sudden whims, and, as usual, could not wait to gratify it. There was nothing to do but go home and hope that she would arrive presently without first getting into some silly scrape.

When she reached home, Louisa went straight upstairs to take off her outdoor garments, pausing at Catherine's room to drop in her sister's parasol, which had been carelessly discarded in the carriage. She placed the parasol on the dressing table, and was turning away when she noticed a crumpled piece of paper lying at her feet. She stooped to pick it up, and her eye chanced on the one word which could be guaranteed to rivet her attention — Oliver's name.

She stood up, wrestling with a desire to read the paper and the guilty conviction that she ought not to do so, as it was almost certainly Catherine's property. After a brief struggle, curiosity won. She smoothed out the creases in the paper, and quickly read its contents.

After she had come to the signature at the end, which she saw with a shock scarcely less sharp than that she had experienced at sight of Oliver's name, she stood for several moments lost in amazement. It seemed from what she had just read that Catherine had been meeting Oliver and that Captain Crendon had been helping her to do so. But why or how such a situation had arisen was quite beyond her.

It was not until she had been standing stock still in the middle of the room for almost a quarter of an hour that it suddenly struck her that here was the explanation for her sister's sudden and furtive departure from the dressmaker's. She had gone to keep the assignation mentioned in the letter.

With this realization, a number of small incidents came flooding back to her memory. Captain Crendon's unexpected call that morning and his invitation to Katie to go driving with him; the remark that Eleanor had bitten off after he had left. Was Nell in the secret, too, whatever it was?

She went downstairs slowly, her mind greatly troubled. She did not quite know what she ought to do. If only Fanny were at home! But she and Eleanor might not return for hours yet, and in the meantime Katie was tearing about the countryside on a clandestine excursion with a gentleman of whom her parents would most certainly not approve.

She was not allowed to brood for long. Presently the butler came into the room and tendered her a card.

"Viscount Pamyngton has called, ma'am. I told his Lordship that Mrs. Hailsham was from home, but he requests the favour of a moment of your time, if quite convenient."

She shook her head. He was on the point of turning away when she changed her mind.

"Stay — I'll see his Lordship. Show him in here."

Had she not been so disturbed herself, she might have noticed that Pamyngton's expression was more serious than usual as he bowed over her hand.

"You will, I trust, forgive me for troubling you, Miss Denham, and especially when you are alone. But I am come on an errand which permits no delay — or at least —" he paused, and now she could see the carefully controlled signs of agitation. "Pray Heaven I may be wrong!" he finished. "Miss Denham, may I ask you a plain question, at the risk of your finding it impertinent?"

"Why — why, yes, I think so —"

"Well then, it is this. Does Mrs. Hailsham know — has she permitted your sister Catherine to drive out of Brighton this afternoon with Captain Crendon, in a closed carriage?"

Louisa's eyes widened. "In a *closed* carriage?"

He nodded. "I saw Miss Catherine stepping into one less than an hour ago, in one of the Lanes." There was a slight hesitation before he went on. "I was on foot, and I followed, for it was perforce going slowly there. I manage to keep fairly close behind until it turned into Church Street, where the driver stopped briefly to pick up Captain Crendon. You may perhaps think my action odd, but I had my reasons — some of them, perhaps, not entirely unknown to you — for following the carriage. I found a hackney and gave chase." A look of chagrin crossed his face. "If only I had had my own horses! They took the London road, and soon outdistanced the hack's broken-down nags, so I was obliged to turn back. I hesitated to call here and to be seeming to pry into what is, after all, no concern of mine — would that it might be!"

She had come to her feet during this speech, so that they were both standing.

"I'm thankful that you did," she said, quietly. "I was almost at my wits' end when you arrived, and meant to seek your counsel, in any case for I have no one else to turn to. My brother-in-law is away from home for a few days and at the moment there is no one but myself — Fanny and Nell are out visiting. And I found this on the floor in Katie's bed-chamber." She held out the crumpled piece of paper. "She's such a sad scatterbrain, she does drop things about, and really I had no right to read it, only that I saw a name —"

She broke off and coloured. "I think you should know that Captain Crendon was here this morning, and Fanny refused to let Katie drive out with him then. She said that John — Colonel Hailsham, that is to say — thought it better for us to have no more to do with him, for he is gambling wildly and getting seriously into debt."

Pamyngton nodded. "He's in the suds, right enough. So do I understand that Miss Catherine —"

Louisa put the paper into his hand. "I think you had better read this," she said.

He scanned it quickly, frowning, then raised questioning eyes to her face. "Do you think this is the explanation?" he asked. "Do you think they've gone to see your friend Mr. Seaton?"

"How can I tell?" she answered, in a bewildered way. "From what's written there, it looks as if Katie and Ol— and Mr. Seaton have been meeting before. But how that came about, or why —"

"I think I can help you there. Miss Catherine confided to me that she had met Mr. Seaton quite by accident when she first went out driving with Crendon. It seems your friend had taken a post in Rottingdean. She also said that they had arranged to meet again at intervals, and that Crendon had agreed to drive her on these occasions."

"But — but why should Oliver wish to meet Katie?"

"I think you know." His eyes softened as he saw her scarlet cheeks. "A man in love is desperate for news of his beloved. Forgive me — I learnt of your unhappy circumstances some time since."

"I suppose Katie told you," Louisa said, in a faltering tone. "She — she really is the most indiscreet —"

"And the most loving, and the most loyal sister any female could desire!" he returned, with some warmth. "She is risking her reputation by allowing Crendon to escort her in this way, but I have no doubt at all that by doing so she hopes to be able to provide some happy outcome for you and Mr. Seaton."

Louisa's eyes filled with tears. "Oh, you are right, sir — she does indeed mean all for my happiness, and I am an ungrateful wretch to criticize her! Indeed, I wonder anyone can love me!"

She lowered her head, and her shoulders shook. Pamyngton flung her the startled glance of any man who is faced with a woman in tears, then moved forward and grasped her hands in a comforting clasp, bending his head towards hers.

"Don't cry, my dear Miss Denham — pray don't cry."

At that moment a voice came from behind them, close to the door.

"And may I ask just what you have done, my Lord, to cause this lady so much distress?"

The very calmness of the tone was menacing.

At the first sound of it, Louisa flung up her head and uttered one choking cry, "Oliver!"

The next moment, she had cast herself into the newcomer's arms.

Chapter XIX: Fear

Catherine did not pause to look about her when she left the dressmaker's premises, but climbed quickly into the waiting carriage. The blinds were drawn, but in spite of the stuffy atmosphere she made no move to push them up and open the windows to let in more air. She chafed inwardly as the vehicle moved slowly along, and felt very tempted to risk a peep outside now and then to see how far they had progressed; but she managed to restrain herself, realizing how important it was that no one should recognize her at present.

After an interval of crawling along at this snail's pace, the carriage pulled up. She shrank into the far corner, turning her face away as the door opened briefly to admit Crendon. He pulled the door to smartly behind him, and the vehicle moved away at a slightly brisker pace.

"So you're here," he stated, in a matter of fact tone. "Did you have any difficulty in getting away?"

"Not the least in the world," she replied, airily. "Louisa was looking over materials in the shop while I was in the back premises being fitted for a new gown. I left a message for her that I'd suddenly thought of a call I wanted to make, and not to trouble to keep the family carriage for me. I waited until the dressmaker had a mouthful of pins before I gave her the message, then I skipped off by the side entrance, which I've often used before. By the time she'd got rid of the pins and gone into the shop to Lou, I was safely in here and away."

"Good. And no one saw you get into the carriage?"

She shook her head. "I couldn't truly say, because I was too intent on getting in quickly. But I think not."

He nodded, and brooded for a moment in silence.

"And now tell me what it's all about," said Catherine.

"You'll have to wait for that until we reach Pyecombe."

She stared. "Why? Surely you must know? Oliver can't have asked you to bring me there to meet him without giving you some reason?"

"The circumstances were difficult. He was with his young charges, and could only snatch a moment or two's conversation with me — sufficient, however, to impress on me the importance and urgency of contriving a meeting between you."

"It is all most odd," she said, wonderingly. "I can't conceive of any circumstances — even though he has got this bee in his bonnet about Pamyngton —"

"What bee is this?"

"Did I not tell you? He believes that Pamyngton is flirting with Lou, and that she may be in danger of taking his attentions seriously. I'm afraid I —"

She broke off, unwilling to admit to Crendon what she had only now come to realize; that she had herself passed on this impression to Oliver, and why. It had been in a moment of pique because Pamyngton had seemed to be paying more attention to Louisa than to herself. The thought shamed her. Was she really such a trivial person as to be swayed by slighted vanity? And what harm might she not have done to Oliver's peace of mind?

Her reverie of self-reproach did not concern her travelling companion.

"Forgive me," he said, casually, "but I'm something short on sleep. If you want entertainment, there are a couple of copies of *The Ladies' Magazine* under the seat. There can be no harm in raising the blind a trifle now."

Thereupon he eased himself comfortably into his corner of the carriage and closed his eyes.

About an hour later, he opened them again.

"We're almost there," he said. "Pull down the blind again. When I leave the carriage remain where you are until I return with your friend."

Catherine started to protest; after an hour in the close confinement of the carriage, she would have been grateful for a breath of fresh air and a stroll. He cut short her protestations summarily.

"This is the main road to London, and it will not do for you to be seen by any passing traveller who might chance to know you. Do as I say, and wait here."

She obeyed reluctantly, her common sense accepting the force of his argument.

He was away for what seemed a long time, but was in fact little more than ten minutes. In the interval, she could hear the horses being changed on their vehicle, and wondered a little that this should be necessary if they were to return directly to Brighton. Perhaps Oliver wanted to go on somewhere else first. She hoped fervently that the whole venture, whatever it might be, could be concluded in time to return her to Brighton for the dinner hour, when she would certainly be missed. Until then, no one was likely to pay much attention to her absence; although when she did eventually return she could expect a sharp scold from Fanny for going off somewhere alone in that way.

To her surprise, Crendon returned alone. He entered the vehicle quickly; it was moving off even as he slammed the door behind him.

"But where is Oliver?" asked Catherine, half rising from her seat,

"Not there. He's had to go on towards London. He left a message for us to follow as quickly as may be."

"Towards *London*?" Her eyes widened. "But I can't possibly go on any farther... if I'm not back by six o'clock, Fanny will make such a stir, you'd never believe! Besides, what on earth can Oliver be at? What does it all mean?"

He raised his shoulders slightly in a negligent shrug as he once more settled into his corner. "How should I know? I am merely doing what he asks, and I recommend that you should do the same."

Perhaps to save any further argument, he shut his eyes again. She watched him for some time in a troubled silence, then flung up the blind on her side with an impatient gesture, staring out at the fields and hedges slipping quickly past. When he uttered no protest, she lowered the window slightly, and gratefully drew in a deep breath of fresh air.

She remained quiet until they had covered another three or four miles. After they had passed through Albourne Green, she leaned forward and touched him on the knee. He opened his eyes at once.

"Captain Crendon — what's the time?"

He pushed up the blind at his side, and inspected his watch. "Not quite a quarter to four."

"But that's absurd!" cried Catherine. "It was turned three o'clock before I managed to slip out of the dressmaker's and we have been travelling now for well over the hour — more like an hour and a half!"

"It probably seems longer than it is," he said, carelessly. "And your dressmaker's clock may have been wrong, anyway."

"No, how could it be, when I was watching the time so carefully so that I might not keep your carriage waiting in the street beyond a quarter past three, as you had requested? I consulted so many clocks on my way there, I should have noticed at once if hers had been wrong!"

"Well, possibly mine may be a few minutes in retard. It doesn't signify."

"But it does! I must be home again for six o'clock at the latest, and to my mind we can only just manage that if we turn back at once! Really, it is a great deal too bad of Oliver. I never before knew him to use anyone in this way. He is in general so thoughtful for others. Where did he say we must meet him?"

"Why can you not leave all to me?" he asked, smiling.

"It's all very well for you to take things so calmly!" she exclaimed, indignantly. "You are not a female, and don't know what it is to be hedged about, and have your every movement questioned!"

"There's a simple solution to that," he said, his smile broadening. "Get married, and then you may do as you please."

"As my husband pleases, you mean," she replied tartly.

He shrugged. "Marry the right man, and he won't trouble you with unwelcome questions. Live and let live — he can be free to go his way, and you yours."

She flung him a contemptuous glance. "I said once before that I don't like your notions. They certainly don't tally with mine on this subject."

"One could scarcely expect it," he said, with a sneer. "You've been reared to the pattern of all genteel females — most likely you nurse romantic yearnings for a chivalrous lover who will spend all his life at your feet. It's not the nature of the beast, my child; and, after a few years of marriage, no one will be more thankful for that fact than you are yourself. You'll see."

"I don't wish to discuss my marriage with you, sir, so kindly hold your tongue on that subject!"

He considered her in an amused way for several moments.

"What a pity," he said, at last. "And it is a subject which concerns me so nearly. Yes, I think I may say that."

From that moment she began to feel uneasy.

Would Oliver really have expected her to come all this way to meet him, without having first given her some very good reason? It was unlike him; and yet he had appeared so moved at their last interview, that almost anything seemed possible. He had spoken as if he intended to see Louisa himself, though. What part could this headlong flight in the direction of London possibly play in a scheme of that kind? A sudden idea came to her.

"Has Oliver gone to my home to see my parents?" she asked, coming out of a reverie that had lasted longer than she realized. "Does he need me to be there for some reason, and so we are to follow him. Is that it?"

She looked expectantly at the Captain, but he had closed his eyes again.

"Oh, pray do answer me!" she cried, stamping her feet in vexation that was not unmixed with anxiety.

She felt the coach slowing. Crendon opened his eyes, muttered an oath, and stuck his head out through the window, impatiently demanding why the driver was stopping.

"Thought as I 'eard ye knock, yer honour," shouted back the coachman.

Catherine, too, stood up and leaned out of the window at her side. In one hand, she loosely held the gloves which she had drawn off some time ago. As the Captain gave the order to start again and the vehicle moved forward with a jerk, the gloves dropped from her hand into the road.

She gave an exclamation of dismay.

"What's amiss?" demanded Crendon.

She told him, and asked him to stop so that she might retrieve her property.

"Oh, pooh! I'll buy you some more," he said, easily. Then in a sharper tone — "You didn't have your initials embroidered on them, by any chance?"

"No," replied Catherine, wondering why he should ask.

He laughed. "Then, they're readily enough replaced, my dear."

She did not like his tone, which was more familiar than anything he had previously used to her. Then, too, her mind would persist in dwelling on his question about the gloves. He had been relieved — yes, it was not too strong a word — to learn that her initials were not embroidered on them. But why? Because they would be easier to replace? That seemed absurd.

It was odd that at this precise moment she should recall her first meeting with Pamyngton, and how she had confided to him — among countless more indiscreet items — that her grandmother considered that she, Katie, had her head screwed on the right way, in spite of her nonsense. Perhaps the protective aura of that old lady, who, though difficult at times, could always be relied upon to pull her grandchildren out of scrapes, reached out to Catherine now. However it was, she suddenly knew without a doubt why Crendon had asked about the gloves. A great many females could, and most probably did, accidentally drop their gloves out of vehicles passing along the road. If found, they would offer no particular clue to their owner. But a glove embroidered with the initials 'C.D.' might seem very significant to anyone searching for a young lady with those initials.

A tremor ran through her. Who was there to search for her? Who could possibly know she was missing until she failed to return at dinner time? Inquiries would be made then, and perhaps the footman might mention that he had taken a note from her to Captain Crendon's lodging. If this information should be pieced together with what Nell knew, or thought she knew, of her sister's relations with the Captain, the family might possibly deduce that she had eloped with him.

Of course, thinking this, they would be anxious to stop it. Any elopement was considered to be in bad taste, let alone one with a penniless man. But who was there to send after her? John Hailsham was away from home; Catherine's father was likewise inaccessible. Not for the first time, she longed for some brothers — officious, interfering brothers who made quite sure that their sisters did not become entangled with the wrong kind of men. Someone like Oliver, who had told her severely that she ought not to be driving around alone with a man whom she knew as slightly as Crendon.

Oliver — of course, they were not going to see him at all. They never had been. It was all a trick. She was not eloping with Captain Crendon, whatever her family might think; but he was eloping with her. Not because he loved her to distraction, either, she thought wryly; but because he wanted her fortune. She herself had told him that it was legally bound to go with her when she married, that her parents could do nothing to stop this.

Suddenly she felt very frightened. Even if her family guessed what had happened to her and tried to send someone to fetch her back, how would they know which way she had gone? She did not know herself where she was going. And she had left no message that could convey any clue — stay, what had she done with the note from Captain Crendon? Was it in her reticule?

She picked the reticule up from the seat beside her and rummaged inside. Her fingers closed on a piece of paper, and she had hard work not to let her expression betray the disappointment she felt.

All was lost. She had brought the note with her.

She glanced covertly at Crendon, but he was not attending to her at that moment, so she cautiously drew the paper out a little way so that she could see the writing on it.

A wave of relief swept over her: it was Mama's writing, not Captain Crendon's. That meant she had left Crendon's note lying about somewhere at home; she only wished she could recall exactly where. Was it likely that anyone might find it, and having found it, read it? Of course they would read anything that might offer a clue to her whereabouts once they knew she was missing. If only she could be sure that they would find it! She was quite certain, at all events, that she had not disposed of it tidily as Louisa would have done, for instance. She reflected wryly on the many hours that had been wasted by various governesses in vain attempts to make her tidy and methodical. What a blessing that they had failed! It might be the saving of her now.

The elation did not last long. She remembered that although Crendon's note had spoken of meeting Oliver at Pyecombe, it had made no mention of going any farther. She remembered that she herself did not know what their ultimate destination might be. At that moment, the vehicle came to a crossroads, and swung right.

Despair gripped her once more. Now they were off the main road, what hope was there that anyone following could find her? She thought of the gloves she had dropped, and an idea came to her.

The window was still open. She leaned towards it, her reticule gripped in her left hand and shielded from Crendon's view.

"What are you doing?" he asked, sharply.

"I–I feel faint…"

She rose, gripping the window sill with her right hand, and quickly dropped the reticule out of the carriage.

"For God's sake!"

He sprang forward, seizing her, and for a moment she feared that he had seen what she had done. He pressed her back into the seat.

"You little fool, you'll get hurt if you stand up when we're travelling at this pace. Sit still, and it will pass off."

He scrutinized her with just a shade of anxiety. The last thing he wanted was a swooning female on his hands, and she certainly looked pale enough. Catherine was quick to sense her advantage. It was small enough, to be sure, but it might serve as a delaying tactic; and what else was a defenceless female to do?

In another few minutes, she had fainted gracefully away.

Chapter XX: Pursuit

"I blame myself," said Oliver, with a troubled look, "I blame myself entirely. How could I have permitted her to run into such hazards to serve my own selfish ends? I feel utterly contemptible!"

"No doubt," replied Pamyngton, as with set lips he sent his racing curricle hurtling along the London road. "But that doesn't help us now, I fear. Pyecombe? Where in Pyccombe, I wonder? We'll try the inn, for a start."

They had lost no time in setting out in pursuit.

When Oliver had appeared at the Hailshams' house, both Louisa and Pamyngton had thought at first that he had brought Catherine home. The discovery that he knew nothing of her whereabouts and had certainly not entrusted Crendon with any message for her, soon led to a correct understanding of events. Without further ado, Pamyngton had announced his intention of going to her rescue. Louisa, half demented with anxiety, had been in no state of mind to argue about the proprieties of this. With both her father and her brother-in-law too far away to help, she was only too thankful to be able to enlist the aid of a gentleman whose family was bound to hers by strong ties of friendship, and in whom, moreover, she personally placed a great deal of trust.

Oliver had been equally insistent that he should accompany Pamyngton, saying that as the whole thing was his fault, he must do something. Pamyngton would have preferred to go alone as he could cover the ground more quickly travelling light; but his kind disposition could not refuse the other man some alleviation in action of his evident remorse, so he agreed.

They were rather more than an hour behind Catherine and Crendon in setting out, but they reached Pyecombe in record time, thus catching up on some of it. Inquiries at the inn were fruitful, as it was not a busy place, and the closed carriage had been remembered. Yes, they had seen a gentleman — dark, brisk, seemed in a hurry — and he had changed horses. They had not seen a lady at all, though what with the drawn blinds, there most likely would have been one. But as to where the carriage had gone next, this they could not say for certain, though it had made off in the direction of London.

"D'you think he's really making for London?" demanded Pamyngton, as he took up the reins again. "This is the most damnable part of the whole business — we've no notion where the devil to look! I've heard he's got some property somewhere to the north of Cuckfield, but no one seems clear exactly where. They said it didn't signify, because in any case it was sure to be mortgaged up to the hilt."

"But he might take her there, all the same, don't you think? I suppose his plan is to marry her, as things are so desperate with him."

It had seemed as though the vehicle was already making all possible speed, but now it shot forward at an increased rate.

"By God!" muttered Pamyngton, between his teeth. "I shall kill him!"

This bloodthirsty statement called forth no reproof from Oliver, who found it most reassuring. It shed light on some points in Pamyngton's past conduct which had previously seemed regrettably obscure to his companion.

"There's nothing to do but to follow this road and ask for them at every inn and turnpike gate we pass," said Oliver, after a minute or two. "I wonder what story he concocted to keep

Katie content to go on with him beyond Pyecombe, where she was expecting to meet me?"

Pamyngton did not answer for a time. Then he said, in a strained voice, "I cannot altogether dismiss the thought that he needed no story — that she may have gone with him willingly."

Oliver Seaton shook his head emphatically. "Louisa was not of that opinion. You heard yourself what she said — that Catherine had declared only this morning that she was not in love with Captain Crendon and never would be."

"How much trust," asked Pamyngton, with a trace of bitterness in his tone, "can one ever place in what any female says on such a subject?"

"Then you think we may be rescuing her from herself, as well as from Crendon?"

"Damned if I know. It's a possibility that has to be faced."

"Our duty is clear, in any event. She can't be allowed to elope with this man, whether she wishes to do so or not. No one who has her interests at heart could think it a suitable match, even if it were to be contracted with traditional propriety, instead of in this hole and corner style."

Pamyngton made no reply to this, but urged the horses on with unremitting zeal. A few miles farther on, he pulled up beside an inn, where Oliver alighted to enquire if anything had been seen of their quarry.

He was back almost at once, and nodded briefly as he swung into his seat. Pamyngton started the horses without further delay.

"Any news? Any hint as to their destination?"

"Nothing. Only that the carriage passed here something less than an hour since. The good woman there says she caught a glimpse of a young lady sitting on the near side of the vehicle and wearing a lilac bonnet. She couldn't say who else was in the carriage, as it went by without stopping, but she was quite definite about the lilac bonnet — trust a female!"

"Yes. Although I saw Miss Catherine stepping into that carriage in Brighton, I certainly couldn't have sworn to the colour of her bonnet. It's as well that Miss Denham took the trouble to tell us what her sister was wearing. Well, for the first time we've had confirmation that she is still travelling with Crendon — not that I supposed otherwise. We must simply press on and hope to catch them. I wish to God we knew exactly what his destination is!"

He was to repeat this after another four miles or so had been covered without their finding anyone who had noticed Crendon's carriage passing that way. They pulled up at the crossroads which they reached soon afterwards. Pamyngton stared hard down the road on their right, which ran to Cuckfield, but could see nothing moving along it.

"Which road to take — on for Handcross, or turn off here?" he asked, despairingly. "Do you realize, Seaton, we're within a few miles now of the Denhams' home?"

"Yes of course I realize it. You most likely don't know, my lord, that I live in the same village."

"I did know, but I'd forgotten for the moment. But do call me Pamyngton, my dear fellow. We'll press on, then? At least there'll be news of them at Handcross, for he'll need to change horses there if he means to go much farther." Once more the curricle sped forward, until they reached another junction a few miles farther along. As before, Pamyngton pulled up briefly to scan the side turning. This time, there was some sign of life; a ploughboy plodding towards them down the dusty road, no doubt returning to his cottage after the day's work.

Pamyngton beckoned the man over to the curricle, and began to question him. After a few moments he broke off, pointing with his whip to something which the labourer was clutching in one hand.

"What have you there?" he asked, sharply.

"Don't rightly know, y'r honour. I found it in the road, just there along." He pointed back the way he had come. "Here, let me look."

Pamyngton reached down and took the object, which was covered in dust.

"It's a lady's reticule, b'God!" he exclaimed, passing it to Oliver. "You don't recognize it, by any chance?"

Oliver turned it over, and shook his head. "No, but we can at least see if it contains anything to show who owns it." He looked at his companion, who nodded; then he drew back the strings of the reticule.

"There's a letter here," he continued, pulling it out. "Possibly — ah!"

"Come on, man! What is it? Is it her property?"

"Undoubtedly. It's a letter from Lady Denham."

"Then they turned off here," said Pamyngton, decisively. He turned to the labourer. "We are acquainted with the owner of this, my good man, and we'll return it. But here's for finding it."

He pressed a coin into the labourer's hand, then turned the curricle expertly and went bowling along the side road.

"I wonder if she dropped that accidentally or on purpose?" he said, thoughtfully.

"On purpose, I would say. It is too much of a coincidence that it should have been dropped just where the road forks."

Pamyngton was silent for a time.

"If that is so," he said, at last, "then she hopes to be followed, and is attempting to guide us. But where to? If only we had any means of finding out!"

"We can't go wrong if we follow this road for the present," replied Oliver. "The problem will be what to do when we reach a turning."

This happened after they had covered about a mile. They pulled up, and Pamyngton jumped down to examine the ground in the hope that Crendon's carriage might have left some tracks. He shook his head as he climbed up again.

"For the life of me, I can't say. Perhaps we had best keep to the main road until we come to some village where we can ask for them. The road runs in the direction of Cuckfield, so it does look as though he's making for this property of his."

Before long, they came to a turnpike gate. As the gatekeeper let them through, Pamyngton asked his question, and was rewarded with the information that a carriage had gone through not half an hour since.

"Do you by any chance know of any property hereabouts owned by a family named Crendon?"

"Oh, ay, that'll be Northlands," replied the gatekeeper. "The old squire died three years agone, and they do say as young 'un games all 'is fortune away."

"How do we reach the house?"

The gatekeeper pointed down the road. "Take first turning left, then after about a mile turn right by Pilbrook Farm. Ye'll see the house nearby, along the lane. But 'tis all shut up — I don't know when young squire was last there. Bain't no manner o' use goin'."

They drove off, and following these directions, reached a small farm standing at the junction of the road with a narrow lane which had grass growing between two deep ruts on each side. Not far along the lane they could see a house of moderate size standing over to the left, in its own grounds.

"We'll leave the curricle here, and finish the journey on foot," said Pamyngton. "Jump down and open the farm gate, will you?"

As Oliver started to obey, a man came out of the cowshed and stood for a moment staring at them.

"We want you to take charge of our vehicle for a while," explained Pamyngton. "We're going up to the house yonder, but that lane's too rough for traffic."

"Going up to the house, are you, sir? Well, now if that don't beat all! Almost a year since anyone set foot in the place and in the space of half an hour a carriage arrives with young squire, and visitors follow him. Likely you're expected, sir?"

"Not precisely," replied Pamyngton. "But will you take charge of my vehicle?"

"Oh, ay, if you desire it. But his carriage went up the lane all right; although," he added, casting his eyes over the light well-sprung curricle and the high-bred horses harnessed to it, "it weren't by any manner of means as dainty a turn-out as this, nor yet the cattle couldn't compare, these being as prime bits o' blood as any man could wish to see in a month of Sundays."

"I'm glad you appreciate them. Obviously I need not scruple to leave them in your care. So Captain Crendon has just gone up to the house, has he? Come, Seaton, we'll follow."

They set off along the road at a brisk pace.

Chapter XXI: Crendon Takes a Tumble

Crendon swore luridly, and putting his head out of the window, signalled to the coachman to stop. Then he pushed open the carriage door and, seizing Catherine from the seat where she was reclining in a much too graceful attitude, bore her inanimate form to the grass verge which bordered the road. Here he set her down none too gently and began massaging her hands.

After a few moments of this treatment failed to bring about any result, he stood up and glowered down at her.

"Hey, you," he called to the coachman, "what the devil do you do to bring females out of a swoon?"

"Ye can leave 'em be — they usually comes round after a bit. Or else loosen their stays," offered the man, helpfully.

A tremor ran through Catherine at this suggestion, but she controlled herself with an effort. It would be time enough to stage a recovery if the Captain looked like acting on it. Meanwhile, the longer she could keep him here, the better. She dared not think what terrors awaited her when they reached their destination, wherever that might be. Even if the note she had left somewhere at home should be found, it might be hours before anyone could come to her rescue. Only her wits would serve her now.

Crendon evidently favoured the first piece of advice that he had been offered, for he left her alone, striding impatiently up and down the road beside the carriage. She half opened her eyes and looked cautiously about her for some means of escape, but found none. There was a hedge quite close to her; but even if she succeeded in getting through it when his back was turned towards her, it would take him no time at all to capture her again. Yet now that she was out of the carriage she had the best opportunity for escape. If only she could think of something! If only someone would come along the road, as Pamyngton had on that unforgettable evening when she had been running away to Brighton. Pamyngton — an involuntary tear escaped her eyelids, and trickled down her cheek.

But no one appeared on the country lane, and very soon she had to shut her eyes tightly, for Crendon was approaching her again. This time he bent over her, raising her head a little, and tried to force some fiery liquid from a flask between her lips. She could no longer keep up her pretence. She sat up abruptly, choking and coughing.

He laughed. "That's better! Shall I carry you to the coach, or can you walk?"

She could say nothing for a moment. He took her hands and attempted to raise her, but she resisted.

"I'm not going in the coach," she said, when she could get her breath back, "at least, not unless we're going straight back to Brighton at once."

"But what about your friend Seaton?" he replied, persuasively. "We've only a few miles to go now, and he's very anxious to see you."

She looked him straight in the eye. "Do you know what I think?" she asked him. "I think you've made all this up about Oliver — I don't believe he ever sent you for me at all!"

"You do, do you?" He stood looking down at her appraisingly for a moment, then suddenly laughed. "Oh, very well, the act has served its turn. Yes, I was fooling you — your clergyman friend doesn't come into this at all, except as a useful excuse for getting you to come with me. Although it's quite on the cards," he concluded, with a sly look, "that I did not need any excuse, and that you would have come willingly."

"You flatter yourself!"

"Naturally you will say so. For an elegant female, there must always be the appearance of modesty."

"I don't think of myself as an elegant female, and I certainly should not carry modesty to such lengths!" retorted Catherine. "Nothing would have induced me to come with you, had I not at first believed that we were to meet Oliver."

"Oh, come, now. Confess that you have a certain interest in me," he said, with a knowing smile.

"Nothing of the kind! I think you are the most detestable, conceited, selfish man it has ever been my misfortune to meet!"

"That's a pity, but it makes no odds. You'll marry me, nevertheless."

She had begun to tremble now, but she gripped her hands tightly together and managed to keep her voice firm.

"That I will not! I'd rather die first!"

He shook his head. "Unfortunately, your death wouldn't serve my purpose. You'll have to defer it until after our marriage."

"You are contemptible!" she said, through white lips. "You only want my fortune."

"Well, yes. But I do quite admire you, and I think we are tolerably well suited. You might go farther and fare worse. You'll find me an easy-going spouse — I'll not interfere with your pleasures, and you must do the same by me."

"You can't force me to marry you, you can't!"

He gave her a pitying smile. "I shan't need to. Your reputation will be in shreds after you've passed a night under my roof. What other course is open to you?"

At this, she leapt to her feet and started to run. He caught her easily and began to drag her towards the coach. In desperation she screamed and screamed, until he placed his hand over her mouth, choking her cries. He half-dragged, half-thrust her into the coach, calling to the coachman, who had been an interested but passive spectator of this scene, to drive onwards.

She collapsed, shaken and breathless, on to the seat.

"You see, it's no use," he said, in a reasoning tone. "You may as well accept the situation."

She was too exhausted and panic stricken to make any reply to this, but sat crouched in her corner, shivering.

Not long afterwards, the carriage pulled up briefly at a toll gate. Crendon moved closer to her.

"Don't scream," he warned her. "I've no wish to manhandle you again."

But for the moment she was past screaming, or, indeed, offering any resistance. The carriage continued on its way until it turned at last along a rough lane. Catherine was shaken and jolted so that once or twice she almost fell from her seat, had not Crendon put out his arm to steady her. The jolting ceased as they turned into a carriage drive, and presently the coach stopped.

"Here we are," said Crendon, alighting, and reaching out to help Catherine down.

She was obliged to take his hand because she was still trembling so much that she would have lost her footing without some support. He escorted her up the crumbling stone steps and, thrusting open a heavy oak door, led her into a cold and musty hall.

"Faugh!" he exclaimed. "The place has gone to rack and ruin — still, it will serve our purpose for a night or two. Now, where's that woman?"

He tugged hard at a bell rope, but it came away in his hand. With an impatient oath, he strode across the floor, opened a door which led to the servants' quarters, and bellowed "Mrs. Samson!"

In a few minutes a little old woman came hurrying out like a frightened mouse.

"Have you obeyed my instructions and made all ready?" he demanded of her.

She bobbed a curtsy. "Yes, sir. Beds are aired and there's victuals enough for two days, like you said. But the house 'bain't 'ardly fit for livin' in, Captain Crendon, on account of me not having the staff to do things proper, like."

"No matter. There's no one here now but yourself, is there?" he asked, sharply.

She shook her head.

"Well, then, take this lady upstairs so that she can freshen up a bit. We'll dine in twenty minutes' time."

"Yes, sir. Please come this way, ma'am."

She led the way up an oak staircase that had once been handsome, and Catherine followed her as if in a trance into a large bedchamber with faded hangings and heavy mahogany furniture. Having shown Catherine where everything could be found, Mrs. Samson vanished for a time, to reappear later with a can of hot water. After setting this down beside the wash-hand stand, she was about to leave for good, but Catherine detained her.

"You must help me — please!" she said urgently, in a low voice. "I must get away from here — Captain Crendon has abducted me!"

"Oh, dear," replied the old woman, in tremulous tones. "Oh, dear, that's very bad, Miss."

"But you will help me, won't you?"

Mrs. Samson shook her head. "I daresn't, Miss; I'd lose my place, and I'm too old now to get another. Besides, he's a shocking temper, has the Captain. You'd not believe."

"But you can't let him do this to me — you're a woman, after all, and you surely can't stand by and see another woman wronged!" exclaimed Catherine, vehemently.

A troubled look came over the thin, lined face. "I wish I could do something, right enough, but I daresn't, and that's an end of it. Bathe your face, Miss, and you'll feel better."

Oddly enough, this lack of support served to put Catherine on her mettle. The weakness which had previously overcome her passed off, and she was ready to make another determined bid for freedom.

"Where is the Captain now?" she asked, in a low tone.

"In his room, Miss, I expect, making his toilet."

"And where is his room?"

Mrs. Samson jerked her head at the wall. "Next door to this."

"Then will you do just this one thing for me?" asked Catherine. "Will you make quite sure that he is safely in his room, then come back and tell me?"

The woman hesitated for a moment, then said, "Can't be any manner o' harm in that, as far as I can see. I could take his hot water in for him."

"Yes," agreed Catherine, eagerly. "But take this, so that you'll be back here more speedily."

She seized the can, and poured a little hot water from it into her own wash basin. Then she offered the can to Mrs. Samson, who took it, and, shaking her head a little, went out of the room.

Once she had gone, Catherine calmly began to bathe her face in the warm water, and felt greatly refreshed by this. While she was drying herself on the towel which had been placed ready, she moved quietly over towards the door, trying to hear what was happening outside.

She heard the door of the next room opening, and a low murmur of voices; but she was unable to distinguish any words. Then the door closed again, and silence followed.

She threw down the towel she had been using, quickly smoothed her hair and donned her bonnet, then stood near the door, waiting.

Mrs. Samson returned in a few moments. She closed the door quietly behind her, and spoke in a whisper.

"He's there, seeing to his toilet and such like. Reckon he won't come out till his dinner's on the table."

"Then you return to the kitchen," directed Catherine, in the same low tone, "and stay there. If I succeed in escaping, you can say that you were too occupied to notice."

The old woman shook her head doubtfully, but she was given no opportunity to remonstrate. Catherine slipped past her through the door, paused for a second on the landing to listen, then sped down the staircase, her light slippers making no sound that could carry through the closed door of Crendon's room. She ran across the hall to the front door of the house; and, seizing the heavy iron handle in both hands, attempted to turn it.

It was very stiff. Panic rose in her as she pulled and wrenched without any effect. Could the door be bolted as well? She cast an agonized glance over its surface. The light was dim, but at last she located the bolts, and saw that they were drawn back.

Mrs. Samson passed behind her at that moment, scuttling for the shelter of her kitchen. Catherine turned the handle again, exerting all the pent-up force of her fear. It yielded with a loud click that sounded in her ears like a clarion call; and, to make matters worse, as the door swung open, it raised a high-pitched note of protest.

She heard the door of Crendon's room open and his voice calling, "What's going on?"

With racing heart, she fled through the open door and down the neglected carriage drive towards the lane. Soon she could hear the crunch of boots on the gravel behind her, and knew with mounting terror that Crendon had started in pursuit. Although she realized that flight was hopeless, that he must surely catch up with her before long, desperation urged her onwards. She must run, run, run, until her legs would carry her no longer, until her lungs burst with the effort...

She heard a shout from in front of her, and now there were more footsteps pounding on gravel; but she did not pause in her headlong flight. Blindly she hurtled onwards, until suddenly she found herself brought to a halt by the haven of protective arms.

"Oh, my love!" said Pamyngton's voice over her bent head. "Here, take her a moment, Seaton!"

She was passed over to another pair of arms, and clung there, gasping pitifully for breath. She heard a sharp crack from behind her; when she had recovered sufficiently to look round, she saw Crendon lying at full length on the drive, a trickle of blood running down his chin, and Pamyngton standing over him, white-faced with anger, his fists still clenched.

Chapter XXII: Catherine Makes a Sacrifice

It was almost an hour later, and Catherine, resilient as ever, felt quite recovered from her recent harrowing experiences. She had wanted to return at once to Brighton, but this Pamyngton had refused to allow.

"I don't think you should undertake a journey of sixteen or more miles after the ordeal you have just been through," he said, firmly. "We are less than half that distance from both your home and mine, and I propose to convey you to either one or the other, as you would prefer." He hesitated, then continued. "I can't help feeling it might be better to take you to Nevern. My mother is a most understanding woman, you know; and after you'd had a night's rest under our roof, she would go with you to your own home and help you to explain everything to your parents."

Catherine inwardly flinched at the thought of explaining her escapade to Mama, and was ready to agree that Lady Nevern would be a most useful ally.

"But what about my sisters?" she demanded, agitatedly. "They'll be waiting for news in Brighton."

"Seaton and I have settled all that," replied Pamyngton, looking at Oliver, who was jogging along beside the curricle on a plough horse hired from the farm. "He's to take a post chaise at the first inn we come to, and with any luck he'll be in West Street in less than two hours."

Catherine had nothing more to say. Everything seemed to have been settled for her, and she was quite content to have it so.

It was not long before they reached a posting inn where they hired a chaise to take Oliver to Brighton. As he was about to step into it, Pamyngton shook hands, and seized the opportunity of having a quiet word with him out of Catherine's hearing.

What he said brought surprise and gratification to Oliver's face.

"I — you are very good," he stammered. "But I really don't see how I could accept — there is no reason why you should do this for me —"

"There's every reason, my dear fellow," murmured Pamyngton, reassuringly. "But for you, I might never have learned in time —" He broke off, his face grim; then he continued, "You may perhaps hesitate to accept an offer of this kind from a mere acquaintance. But it would make a difference, would it not, if we should chance to be distantly related — say, by marriage, for instance?"

Oliver grinned, and made Catherine an elaborate bow. "I thought the wind lay in that direction," he said, as the post chaise moved off.

"What did Oliver mean?" she asked, as Pamyngton handed her up into the curricle.

"Oh, nothing to signify," he answered, carelessly.

There was silence for a time. Catherine realized that they were now travelling along that same road where she had first met him; and a host of memories came crowding back to her, shutting out completely the more recent unpleasant events which concerned Captain Crendon.

"I trust it will not put out Lady Nevern to have an unexpected guest thrust upon her in this way," she said, politely.

"My mother is never put out by anything. She is possessed of a most equable disposition. And, of course," he added, with calculated audacity, "she will be delighted to welcome you when she learns that I am going to marry you. It is a scheme on which she has long set her heart."

Catherine gasped. "I — you — whatever are you saying? How can you jest on such a subject?"

He gave her a long, serious look, which brought the colour to her cheeks.

"I am not in jest, Katie. I was never more serious in my life."

"Then you take too much for granted, sir!" she retorted, tartly.

"Oh, yes, I realize that. I would have to be far more conceited than I hope I am, to feel that you had ever offered me the slightest encouragement. On the contrary, you have frequently told me that you detest me, and never wish to see my face again."

"And you deserved it, when I said those things!" she answered, in a censorious tone.

"I do not deny it," he replied, humbly — almost too humbly, she felt, looking suspiciously at him to see if a smile was lurking in his eyes.

"Oh, very well," she said, "I forgive you, and I acknowledge that your odious spying upon me turned out for my own good, in the end. But do not take too much upon yourself, sir!"

"I promise that I won't. But all the same, I have great hopes of persuading you to marry me. You see, I rely upon your devotion to your sisters, which I have so often noticed in the past."

She turned towards him with wide opened eyes. "My devotion to my sisters —?"

"Allow me to explain. Do you recall that on the occasion of our first meeting I told you that I was related to a Bishop, to establish my bona fides, as it were?" She nodded, still looking puzzled. "Well, I have just offered your friend Seaton a comfortable living which is vacant in my uncle's See."

Her face lit up at once, and she placed her hand impulsively on his arm.

"Oh, no, truly? How splendid — how very, very kind of you! This will mean that Oliver can wed Lou at last — how happy they will be!"

"So I thought myself, but there's a slight hitch," he said, solemnly.

"Why, whatever could that be? If Oliver only has a comfortable income of his own — and you did say it was a good living —"

"A most wealthy one, in fact," he affirmed. "That is not the cause of the trouble. The fact is, your friend Seaton is a very independent man, and cannot bring himself to accept what he chooses to think of as a favour from someone with whom he is little more than acquainted."

"Oh, if that isn't just like Oliver!" she exclaimed in disgust. "He is so proper, it's quite incredible!"

"But there is a way round his difficulty, you see," explained Pamyngton, looking into her eyes. "And that is what I meant when I spoke of relying on your sisterly devotion. If Seaton and I were connected by marriage, for instance —"

A slow smile was spreading over her face.

"You see how it is, Katie. You will be obliged to sacrifice yourself for your sister Louisa's sake."

"What was it Mr. Eversley called you?" she asked. "A smooth customer — how right he was!"

Her hand had dropped away from his arm, but he found it with his left one, keeping the reins in his right.

"I know my faults are legion, but will you take me, in spite of them?" he asked, in a quiet, serious tone.

She turned her head away, unable to answer for the moment.

"Forgive me," he said, in a contrite tone, "after all you have suffered today, the last thing you must be wanting to hear is a declaration of love."

Catherine could think of nothing she would rather hear from Pamyngton, at any rate, but she did not mean to say so. She puzzled her wits for some way of encouraging him to continue without revealing her intense interest in the subject.

He mistook her silence for agreement, and said no more, but sighed gently and released her hand. They continued for some time in this way, sitting side by side without speaking. Occasionally he would steal a glance at her face, and then he would sigh again. At last, she decided to take pity on him.

"You know," she said, reflectively, "I was quite certain that you were falling in love with Lou."

"No, how could you possibly think that?" he asked, in amazement.

"I was not the only one to have that impression," she reminded him. "You did take her hand in a most amorous way in full view of everyone at the Pavilion musical party, after all."

"But that was merely a gesture of comfort," he protested. "Your sister was upset by the song — I should have been a brute indeed not to have responded to such distress, especially as I myself knew —"

He broke off, reluctant to finish what he had been about to say.

"You would say," she concluded for him, "that you knew what it was to be unhappy in love?"

He nodded. "I felt deeply for your sister, as anyone must who has ever suffered from a like cause."

"So it was no more than sympathy? But she was always singing your praises, you know. I told Oliver of it, and that's what made him so concerned to discover exactly what your intentions towards her might be."

"My intentions — towards your sister? Upon my word, in my anxiety not to wear my heart upon my sleeve, I seem to have created a totally false impression all round! As for her praising me, I think it sprang from that fellow feeling between us which I have mentioned. She guessed what my feelings were for you, and hoped to change your hostile attitude towards me. No one who knew Miss Louisa could ever doubt her unswerving attachment to Seaton."

"And what about you?" She had not meant to say this, but some little flicker of jealousy flared up for a brief moment. "You, too, once had an unswerving attachment. Yet now you say that I have taken her place —"

He turned quickly towards her, his eyes deep with feeling. She caught her breath; and suddenly they both knew that there could be no more pretence.

"No," he said, quietly. "You have your own place in my heart. It never has, and never could, belong to anyone else. I love you, Katie, and want you for my wife."

"But how can you, after all I hear about her?" she asked, in unaccustomed humility. "She was an acknowledged belle, a famous horsewoman, and I don't know what besides! Whereas I —" she smiled reminiscently — "oh, you know I can't even stay on the back of a donkey for five minutes; and what's worse, I am for ever getting myself into some stupid scrape or other."

"That's why I love you, dearest. Georgiana was a strong-minded woman, who had no real need of me. But even if you can't bring yourself to love me," he said, with a smile, "at least I can occasionally be of use to you by standing by to help you out of scrapes."

"When did you first know that — you loved me?" she asked, shyly.

"Why, when you told me that it was all planned for you to marry me, of course!" he replied, laughing.

"Oh!" She wrinkled her nose at him. "You are too bad, to remind me of that!"

Reluctantly, he gave his attention to the road for a moment. When he turned to her again, his expression was serious once more.

"Is my case quite hopeless?" he asked, diffidently. "If I wait —"

She smiled up at him, her expressive eyes soft and glowing.

"Oh, you must know by now I can never wait for anything! Besides, I've waited quite long enough — ever since you sent me those roses, I have known that I meant to have you — dear Pamyngton."

She spoke the last words in a whisper.

It was fortunate that the horses were not fresh, otherwise they might have taken advantage of the sudden slackening of their normally expert driver's control.

A NOTE TO THE READER

If you have enjoyed the novel enough to leave a review on **Amazon** and **Goodreads**, then we would be truly grateful.

Sapere Books is an exciting new publisher of brilliant fiction and popular history.

To find out more about our latest releases and our monthly bargain books visit our website: **saperebooks.com**

Printed in Great Britain
by Amazon